To Gether Tales

Richard Seltzer

ALL THINGS
THAT MATTER
PRESS

To Gether Tales

ISBN: 9781737767176

Library of Congress Control Number: 2022933923

Cover Design by All Things that Matter Press

Cover ship photo by ray-harrington-Y2V0ph_3_qY-unsplash.jpg

Published in 2022 by All Things that Matter Press

To my wife Barbara (1950-2012)

Acknowledgements

Thanks to:

Rex Sexton and his widow Rochelle Cohen,
Diane Motowidlo, and
Nancy Felson
for helpful feedback and encouragement,

Gabi Coatsworth for her monthly Writers' Rendezvous meetings,

Phil and Deb Harris at All Things That Matter Press for excellent editing,

And my son Bob for his generous support.

What Has Been Lost

"Gather ye rosebuds while ye may,
Old Time is still a-flying
Tomorrow will be dying"
~ Robert Herrick

May 2020

"Gather ye rosebuds ..." That snippet of poetry means something more today than it did when Herrick wrote it. Yes, of course, we age and die, and each year seems to go by faster than the last. But now, in addition to that, we know that the world itself can change suddenly. Everything is transitory, not just us.

I'm alone now, and billions of others are either alone or in small family groups due to *social distancing,* That two-word contradiction should be the stuff of dystopic science fiction set in the far future after civilization fell apart. Instead, it's part of everyday life.

I don't know if this plague, like the ones that came before, will pass, and life will return to the *old normal,* or if there's no going back.

Twice before, in my lifetime, mankind went through what felt like no-going-back changes. The Viet Nam War combined with domestic upheaval and the oil embargo changed our perceptions and priorities. Likewise, the attacks on 9/11 changed how we viewed the present and the future. But life went on. Within a few years, it was as if those events had never occurred.

I'm reminded, too, of London during the Blitz, as recorded in novels and movies, how quickly people adapted to a *new normal,* millions living with the daily threat of random imminent death, feeling empathy and responsibility not just for family and friends, but also for the strangers around them. But when the war ended, they, too, returned to their *old normal.*

I hope that will be the case this time as well. But we may not be so lucky. A few years from now, looking back, pre-pandemic and post-pandemic may seem far apart. Something may be lost, with nothing gained.

Now, in the midst of it, not knowing the eventual outcome, I look back a few years, with nostalgia, to a time that may never return — the good old days, the Golden Age, a time when daily life was much simpler.

A recent headline read: "Satellite images show armadas of vacant cruise ships huddling together at sea." Ships clustered and circling in the Atlantic. From far above, they looked like a school of dying whales. Those ships weren't riding out a storm. No port had dock space to accommodate them, nor would any port welcome them, bringing the dread contagion that had spread rapidly on shipboard, with the world watching news videos as they were turned away, repeatedly, and forced to wander. With no passengers, just skeleton crews who have no place to go and no way to get there, such ships, some of which cost more than a billion dollars to build, are still in holding patterns, in the hope that the pandemic will end and that they will go back to business. But this may be the end of that industry and the way of life it supported.

It's against that backdrop that I remember and record a many-storied cruise from two years ago. On a cruise, strangers could be thrown together around the same dinner table for the duration, seven days or two weeks or all the way up to the ultimate — a world cruise of a hundred eleven days. This was a seven-day Eastern Caribbean cruise on the Regal Princess, a floating town, with thirty-five hundred passengers and thirteen hundred crew. This time, by chance, my dinner companions were articulate, creative, and fun. One among us, Uncle Adolph, served as ringmaster, coaxing us to tell our personal stories and then to create new stories which kept us entertained and bonded us together with our knowledge of and concern for one another.

Of course, at the time, none of us had the least suspicion that the world we took for granted would soon change, that the tales that we shared over dinner might soon seem like fairy tales, impossible in the harsh conditions of a *new normal.*

I treasure those stories now as I remember and record them, trying with my words to preserve the romantic flavor of that bygone age, the hopes and desires that once shaped lives and that now seem unreal. I didn't know at the time that human nature could change so much, that we could adapt so quickly to survive not just contagion but economic disruption as well, and that that might mean the end of hopes and dreams, and the end of what we once thought of as *romantic love.*

I don't want to imply that cruises by nature were romantic, à la *Love Boat.* These stories, for the most part, are not about shipboard romance. The ship is the setting for the telling of the tales, not necessarily the setting of the tales themselves. I'm not just lamenting the end of cruising. The loss is far greater than that. Romantic love itself may have ended — God forbid.

I should start by introducing my fellow travelers, describing them and sketching their backstories and having them talk about their life experiences. Instead, I'll start with a story that, for me, epitomizes the reason for me writing this book.

For those who like an orderly predictable narrative, the teller of this first story was Beth, and she told it on Day Five. But the story stands on its own and makes clear my sense of change and loss.

Let Beth begin.

Beth: The Princess Tango

Alex and Laurel got engaged before their first date. His best friend and her best friend got married. They were both in the wedding party. He gave her a ride home. She invited him in. He proposed immediately, and she accepted without hesitation. They went on a Caribbean cruise for their honeymoon, on the Princess ship that was the set for *The Love Boat* TV series.

They were deliriously happy together. Neither of them had danced much before the cruise, but they wound up going to free dance lessons in the afternoon and then dancing from dinner to midnight, every night.

The dance instructor and his wife were Chinese. He claimed that he had taught finance at the Harvard Business School and that this was his retirement — cruising the world with his wife, who was his dance partner, and passing on to others these steps that for them had led to marital harmony and bliss. "Happy wife, happy life," he said proudly.

He was rigid in his teaching style: 'One, two, three, four. One, two, three four. This is how it is done in the cha cha ... This is how it is done in the merengue ... This is how it is done in the tango ... This is the way. This is the sequence of moves and steps and no other. If you and your partner each learn that and do that, you will be in sync with one another and will experience the joy of dance and the joy of marital harmony.'

At first, Alex and Laurel rigidly followed his instructions. But they soon found that their bodies moved together naturally, even when they forgot the instructions, even when they unintentionally used a cha cha move in a foxtrot, even when they mimicked other experienced dancers and added unorthodox side steps and hand-over-hand twirls. By Day Four, they stopped going to the lessons, but still danced until midnight, and their repertoire expanded. They felt the music in their bodies, and they anticipated one another's moves with no effort at all. Soon their dancing evolved to a set of moves that they could, with minor modifications, use to any music from waltz to tango.

There was one routine they chanced upon that they hadn't seen anyone else do — one, two to the left, overhead twirl with handholding, twirl back again, side left, side right, then walk straight ahead with arms joined behind their backs. They were proud of that move and did it smoothly. Other couples would stop and watch when they did it, and then would try to imitate it.

That cruise, that magical moment, ended all too soon.

They flew back to Philadelphia, picked up their car at the airport, and drove toward their home in Huntingdon Valley. It was a clear moonlit night in June. They were holding hands and listening to a radio station playing *The Tennessee Waltz*, which they had danced to as the ship sailed away from St. Martin, when a tractor trailer coming toward them on the other side of the road lost control and jack-knifed into them.

When Alex woke up in the hospital, he was told that Laurel had died in the crash. At first, in his confusion, he didn't know who Laurel was. His parents and his sister helped fill in the gaps in his memory, but he couldn't help but feel that he was dreaming now—that this was a nightmare that he would wake up from, or that he had dreamt meeting Laurel and falling in love with her and had dreamt their cruise-ship honeymoon. Nothing felt real — not the past, not the present.

Eventually, he went on with his life. He married again. They had two kids. They divorced. He married again and had another kid and divorced. His memories of Laurel and their time together faded.

When he retired, forty years after the accident, he treated himself to a Caribbean cruise, alone.

Retirement was a downer. Living alone was a downer. His kids were grown and married with kids of their own and were scattered, living hundreds of miles from Philadelphia. He saw them once, sometimes twice a year. And, aside from his kids, he had little to look back on with pride, and nothing to look forward to. The routine of going to work and doing what was expected of him was over. He was no longer part of the work-related web of expectation, recognition, and camaraderie. When he jogged or used a treadmill at the gym, as his doctor recommended, he couldn't help but feel that all the activity of his life had been like this — going in circles or going nowhere, accomplishing nothing that would last. When he died, aside from his kids, he would leave nothing behind, no sign of his existence. He might just as well have never lived.

Going down to dinner on Day Two of the cruise, as they were sailing away from Princess Cay in the Bahamas, a band in the Piazza was playing *The Tennessee Waltz* and a dozen couples were dancing to it. He overheard two couples talking about an unusual dance move that one couple had done on Day One and that nearly all the experienced dancers had picked up. It resembled a tango move, but they used it in the cha cha, the merengue, and even the waltz, like now. They called it the *Princess Tango Step*. There was a legend that had been passed down through the years about a young couple on their honeymoon who had first done it and done it so well that others copied it and others copied them. People called it a *meme*, a piece of culture that perpetuates itself, an echo of that time long ago and of the love of that couple who first danced it, as if the love of two people in harmony with one another found natural expression in these very moves, and as long as there was love in the world there would be the *Princess Tango*.

That's what Beth said. The way she told that tale stuck in my imagination, together with the sadness, and the bitter-sweet consolation that the dance continued, that there would be the *Princess Tango*. But now we know that cruise ships may never sail again, or if they do, restrictions will apply. Passengers will wear masks, gloves, and maybe complete protective suits. There will be no public ballroom dancing. There will be no *Princess Tango*.

Also, if Alex and Laurel had been masked and gloved and dressed for safety, if they couldn't see the expressions on one another's faces, couldn't feel a tingle when their fingertips touched, couldn't exchange flashes of unguarded attraction, would they have ever fallen in love? Would anyone? Will there ever again be love-at-first-sight?

Sharing our tales over dinner, we believed that romantic love would always be a possibility for people of all ages. But perhaps, subconsciously, we sensed the fragility of that belief. Perhaps we were moved to share these stories, in part, because of the possibility that emotional magic might someday go away. Not that people would never love again, but that they wouldn't be able to fall in love simply and spontaneously.

We celebrated love in all its forms, from the sweet innocence of youth to the uninhibited lust of age, with a sprinkling of bawdy wit.

And I want to capture and preserve the flavor of that time as well as the stories themselves.

Day One:

Leaving Fort Lauderdale

Beth and Harry: Loominus

On the first night, three couples and I were seated at a table-for-eight near the windows on the port side of the Regal Princess as Fort Lauderdale faded into the distance. This was the first night of our seven-day Eastern Caribbean cruise. I was scanning the dining room, hoping to spot and catch the eye of Rinaldo, our Filipino waiter, wanting him to hurry up and deliver my baked Alaska or I'd miss the opening-night show, which would include a comedy team, imitators of Abbott and Costello.

The seven of us were talked out. Our introductions hadn't uncovered any mutual acquaintances or common interests, so we bragged about the cruises we'd been on, shared memories and rumors about ships and cruise lines. We had nothing more to say to one another. The random sounds of silverware and plates and the cacophony of voices from other tables invaded our awkwardly silent space. What a waste of time, waiting for dessert, after having sat at this table for nearly two hours already, and about to miss the show. The cruise itself was a waste. Why had I signed up for it? Yet another forgettable week in paradise, that I might just as well have spent alone in Connecticut.

When I spotted Adolph, I thought he was a crew member, an entertainer meant to divert passengers impatient with the slow service.

He was wearing a straw hat, and no one wore hats anymore, except baseball caps on deck on sunny days, certainly not in the dining room. His white suit looked like a costume from a nineteen-forties movie, maybe a minor character like Peter Lorre, entering Rick's in *Casablanca*. As he got closer, from his girth, bulbous nose, and red cheeks, he could have been a W. C. Fields impersonator.

All eyes followed him in a wave of silent shock that spread in his wake as he walked through the dining room, led by Rinaldo. Adolph relished the attention, taking off his hat to wave it at his astonished audience, before settling into the chair to my right, wriggling to arrive at a comfortable position, then once again donning his hat, with a flourish and a smile.

"Welcome, ladies and gentlemen," he addressed our table. "I'm glad you could join me here. My name is Adolph. You can call me Uncle Adolph. Everybody does."

The entire dining room of five hundred people was silent, all eyes trained on him, dreading what he might do next to break the norms of polite society.

"Rinaldo," he said, reading the waiter's name tag and handing him back the menu, "I'll have the beef Wellington, please—rare, very rare, a rare delight, I'm sure; and a glass of cranberry juice, if you could. Thank you."

Beth, who would eventually tell the *Princess Tango* story, sat across the table from Adolph and me. She was in her early thirties, with hair dyed bright red and green. That first night, she wore a plaid jacket and matching skirt, giving her the look of an unaffected and unselfconscious teenager, in sharp contrast to the garish color of her hair.

Her husband, Harry, took no notice of her hair, which told me that it wasn't a passing whim. For her, that was normal. Harry sported a two-day growth of whiskers, neatly trimmed. He hadn't forgotten to shave. This was his look, harder to maintain than close-shaving or a beard. His was a manly, deliberately relaxed look. His clear blue eyes were opened wide with curiosity and innocence, the look of someone from a small town having come to a big city and looking at strangers unguardedly. But his confident manner seemed to imply that he was not new to the city and its ways. He knew his way around, but he consciously chose to maintain his small-town openness.

The pair of them looked like they belonged together, even in the moments when they weren't holding hands or looking into one another's eyes. Their temperaments were in harmony, and even in their slightest gestures, they moved as if in awareness of the presence and mood of the other. When, over the course of the cruise, he or she told romantic tales, they spoke with conviction. They believed in love, based on their personal experience.

As soon as Adolph had comfortably settled his expansive behind in the normal-sized chair, he challenged Beth, having no qualms about insulting and provoking her. His first words to her were, "What's with the crazy hair, young lady?"

She shot back, "On my planet, this is natural. Like your hat is natural on yours."

Her husband spoke up and explained for her, "Beth has wild hair color because she's shy. That's camouflage. She wants everybody to focus on her hair, not look her in the eye. That's her way of hiding in plain sight. She learned that trick from Lainie, a lady from Perth, Australia, who we met on our first cruise together. Beth asked Lainie what no one else dared ask, what you just asked, 'Why the crazy hair?' She got that explanation of camouflage and embraced it as a strategy for herself.

"When I met Beth, she was a natural redhead and wore her hair long, letting it cover half her face. That was another kind of disguise. She was standing in front of a dress shop, looking at her reflection in the window. She pushed her hair to the side, to get a better look at herself, and by accident, at that moment, I was standing behind her, looking at that same window. Our eyes met in the reflection, and her eyes opened wide, unguarded. That's the moment I fell in love with her."

"Now, wait a minute," Beth interrupted. "That isn't how we met. Why are you making up a story for this stranger?"

"Why not make one up?" Adolph chimed in. "I love a good story. Sir, what's your name?"

"Harry."

"Ah. Prince Harry to my Falstaff. Tell me more of your tale. Where were you and why were you there, and why does she remember it differently?"

Beth sat bolt upright, staring at her husband in disbelief, oblivious of the baked Alaska that the waiter had placed in front of her, that she had been anxiously awaiting and that was now melting.

Harry continued, "I was an American tourist strolling through Edinburgh. I was unattached and wanted to be attached. I was looking at young ladies and imagining what it would be like to spend a lifetime with this one or that. I had just arrived. I had accumulated vacation time, but barely enough to tramp through Europe the way I had wanted to since college days. When I chanced upon Beth, I was trying to find my hotel, checking my map, checking the street signs, lost in the maze of twisting hilly roads. Our eyes met briefly in their reflection in the window. Her look was open, welcoming, like we already knew one another. I flinched. She laughed. I hurried on, still looking for my hotel. Once I had checked in, I rushed back, hoping to find her again. I got lost and had to ask for directions half a dozen times before I found my way back to the hotel, the Courtyard Marriott, near the Omni Center on Greenside Row. I had intended to stay in Edinburgh for just a day or two. I ended up staying for weeks, looking for her."

Beth looked at him quizzically, "You mean the first time we talked was the second time you saw me?"

"The third time," he corrected her. "I also spotted you coming out of the Cosmo, that buffet restaurant at the Omni Center. You were in a wedding party, probably a shower. Everybody wore white sashes with labels in big letters — *Bride, Bridesmaid, Mother-in-law-to-be*. Yours read *Friend who didn't get picked as bridesmaid*. Before I got up the courage to approach you, you climbed into a limo with the others and vanished into the night."

"This is all nonsense," Beth explained to the others at our table. "We met for the first time in the hand-woven clothing shop where I worked, on the Royal Mile, near Holyrood Palace."

Harry continued, "I was shopping for a scarf to send home to my sister. This shop girl caught my eye. She stood pigeon-toed, knock-kneed, shoulders bent, shy, retiring, self-conscious. When I addressed her to ask for prices, she pushed her long red hair to the side, revealing her freckles and dimples. Her nose curved up, gradually, smoothly, like a ski-jump for beginners. She pulled her shoulders back, smiled, and opened her eyes wide. Green eyes, the same eyes I had seen reflected in that shop window weeks before. She was the girl I had been looking for, the woman I'd been looking for my entire life. She was luminous, and I told her that, punning on the word *loom*. She told me that yes, some of these scarves were imported from America, handwoven by a company named Loominus.com in Woodstock, New York. I laughed, then bought one and asked her to show me how it should be worn. Then I asked her if we could take the scarf for a walk together. We spent the rest of the day swapping life stories while strolling through Edinburgh Castle. A week later, she flew back with me to New York. Three months later, we married."

"That's the real story," Beth confirmed. "We wrote our own vows, 'You'll be my warf and I'll be your weft. And we'll weave together the threads of our lives.'"

"Yes, that's the real story, but it's not the whole story," Harry corrected her. "Our eyes did link in our reflections in a shop window weeks before that, and I did see her at that party at the Cosmo."

Adolph added, "I'd wager you were connected before that, as well."

"What do you mean?" asked Beth.

"I sense it in his eyes and in his voice," Adolph continued. "I have a feel for when a story is just a sketch, when there's more to be revealed and explained."

"Well?" Beth turned to Harry. "What more haven't you told me? Or what more about us do you choose to invent for the amusement of strangers?"

"ITP," Harry replied. "I've told you about that, Beth. The blood condition I have. Immune thrombocytopenic purpura. A low platelet count. If the count gets too low, my blood won't clot properly, leading to excessive bleeding, like hemophilia."

Beth interrupted, "You're not going to deliver your rant about the Russian Revolution, are you?"

"Please do!" Adolph interjected. "I love rants."

Beth objected, "What does this have to do with me and you, with us meeting, with our love story?"

"Let me tell it the way it needs to be told, with all its twists and turns."

"If you must," she conceded.

"It began with my father's stroke."

"So now you're going to say that we met because of your father's stroke?"

"It takes lots of threads ..."

"To make a village?"

"Exactly. And this thread began with my Dad. He was fifty. He had sudden acute dizziness. Two bouts of it, a day apart. He went to the doctor, and then to the hospital for an MRI. The film showed a big black spot on his cerebellum. He was lucky that there was no measurable deficit. He was as he had always been. But the next time something like that happened he probably wouldn't be so lucky, and the next time could come soon. They couldn't find a clot, but the doctor presumed there must have been one, and prescribed coumadin, a blood thinner.

"I was in college at the time, researching a paper on the Russian Revolution, and using the Web to track down details about Rasputin, the notorious peasant priest whose influence on the Czar was one of the factors leading to disaster. That influence was based on his seemingly magical ability to treat Alexis, the heir apparent, who had hemophilia, the bleeding disease that was also known as the *royal disease*, because so many of Queen Victoria's descendants had it. No one doubted that Alexis, a great-grandson of Victoria, had that condition, and there was no medical treatment for it. He bruised easily, and a bruise on any part of his body could trigger the swelling of internal bleeding, threatening his life. Rasputin, for no known medical reason, was able to stop the bleeding, and on several occasions was credited with saving the child's life.

"On the Web, I found stories about Rasputin's orgies with wealthy and noble ladies and stories about his demonic powers. Purportedly it was almost impossible to kill him. But what caught my attention was an article that questioned the diagnosis of hemophilia.

"That was when I first learned about ITP. The bleeding of hemophilia is due to a deficiency of a clotting factor; and, in the early twentieth century, there was nothing that could be done to treat that condition. In contrast, the bleeding of ITP is due to a low platelet count, and the count can fluctuate from normal to dangerously low and back again. If Alexis had ITP and not hemophilia, his condition would come and go, rather than be persistent. And if Rasputin were lucky enough to be on the scene when the count was going up, he would be credited with the cure. Hence the Russian Revolution may have been caused, in part, by a misdiagnosis."

Beth asked, "What does that have to do with the price of sheep in Glasgow?"

"When Dad had his stroke and his doctor couldn't find a clot, this article was fresh on my mind. I had a hunch that his stroke hadn't been caused by a clot. Maybe it was due to internal bleeding, in the brain. Maybe Dad had ITP. In that case, blood thinner could kill him. I insisted that he be tested, and it turned out that indeed he had a low platelet count. The doctor took him off the coumadin and put him on blood pressure medicine instead. He's been doing fine ever since."

Beth insisted, "How does that relate to you and me meeting in a hand-woven shop in Edinburgh?"

"My doctor said that ITP isn't hereditary, but I had a hunch he was wrong. I got tested, and I had it too. My count was much lower than Dad's, dangerously low; so I was given gamma globulin treatments."

"What?" asked Beth.

"That's the same treatment they give to expectant mothers, if the father and the mother have different Rh factors."

"Please get to the point."

"I went to the hospital, to the Oncology and Hematology Department, once a week, and, for hours, I had slow-drip intravenous treatments. On either side of me sat cancer patients getting chemo. That's how I met the lady who saved your life."

"What?"

"Let me explain. By chance, she and I sat next to one another three weeks in a row. Others listened to music, lost in their own worlds, oblivious to everything and everyone. She smiled at everyone who entered the room and greeted them. She was reading *Finnegan's Wake* and chuckling at the puns like it was a joke book. She said with a laugh. 'Whether it's a one liner or a shaggy dog story, life is a joke. Enjoy it while you can.'

"She and I talked about our medical conditions, our families, our lives, and our hopes. She had Hodgkin's lymphoma. She had found out about it early, so her prognosis was excellent. Her husband deserved the credit. He had noticed a swelling at the base of her neck and insisted that she see a doctor. She had hair down to her waist, and she joked that she'd probably lose it all from the chemo. I joked that when it grew back, she should dye it bright red and green. Fortunately, she made a full recovery. She and her husband moved to Perth, Australia, and bought a sheep farm. That was twelve years ago, when I was in college."

"You're kidding?" Beth asked. "You've got to be making this up?"

"That was Lainie."

"And when we met her on our first cruise together, the two of you never let on that you knew one another before?"

"That was fun."

"And now? You tell me this now?"

"This is fun too. You see, if I hadn't met Lainie, I would never have noticed the swelling at the base of your neck, and you wouldn't have had chemo."

"And I wouldn't have crazy hair."

"And we wouldn't be cruising to celebrate your recovery."

"That's how you got that hunch and sent me to the doctor?"

"Yes, and you could say I fell in love with you on a hunch. Subconsciously, I must have noticed the swelling at the base of your neck that day we met in the scarf shop. I must have been drawn to you in part because I sensed your vulnerability and knew we were meant to be together. My Dad having his stroke, me researching Rasputin, me having ITP, and me meeting Lainie when she was getting her chemo, all led to your cure, which led to us being on this cruise, and telling our tale at dinner. The threads of fate all come together."

"Bravo!" exclaimed Adolph. "I love the weaving metaphor. One thread of story, then another, back and forth. You're a natural storyteller."

Thelma and Stan: Graveside Romance

"Carpe diem is what I say," noted the lady sitting to Adolph's right.

"And you are, madame?"

"Thelma. We're Thelma and Stan. I always say, like the ice cream shop at our local mall, 'Life's short. Eat dessert first.' I have a koi, a carp, a Japanese goldfish. I've had him for sixty years, and he's two and a half feet long. I call him 'Carpe Diem'. He's my reminder — not a memento mori, a reminder of death, rather a memento vivendi, a reminder that it's time to live, that it's always time to live."

"A wise woman," noted Adolph. "A woman after my own heart."

Thelma was rosy-cheeked and of generous proportions. Dieting would be contrary to her self-indulgent style of life. The extra flesh on her face erased what on a thinner woman would be wrinkles. And she dressed to draw attention to her fulsome bust. At over eighty, she had a youthful glow and an unabashed manner of speech. Her husband's evident delight at her looks and style amplified her aura of mature sexuality. She frequently stroked his thigh or kissed the lobe of his ear, telegraphing to him and to all around that she was ready to pleasure him as soon as dinner was done.

They were the same height, about five foot six, but she was about fifty pounds heavier than he. They could have dressed up as Laurel and Hardy, with him as Stan Laurel. That made it easy to remember that his name was Stan. And her name was easy to remember as well. No one else at the table was old enough to be named *Thelma*.

"We're newlyweds," she announced proudly. "I'm his first. He's my eighth. We're going to enter the *Newlywed Game* tomorrow. We've got our answers figured out and rehearsed."

"How does that work?" asked Adolph,

"The MC asks the husbands questions with the wives out of the room. Then he brings in the wives and asks them the same questions. If you give the same answers as your spouse, you win."

"And what, may I ask, are your answers and the questions thereunto?"

"They always ask, 'When did you do it last?' To that we'll answer, 'This morning.' Then they ask, 'What's the most unusual place you've done it?' To that we'll say, 'On the balcony.' That'll get the audience laughing. We're a shoe-in."

"You tell it like it is." Adolph chuckled.

"I'm no someday-school teacher, that's for sure."

"You sound like my ex."

"You're divorced?"

"Never married. She died three months ago. Mae, I called her. You don't resemble her physically. But your style reminds me of her."

"I'm honored by the comparison but sorry for your loss."

"Yes, three months ago," Adolph repeated, turning solemn and serious, "after thirty years of almost-married bliss. She was Mae Estes, Mae East not West, and never the Mark Twain shall meet. But enough of me," he smiled again. "How did you newlyweds meet?"

"Through Match," said Thelma.

"No," Stan interrupted, taking her hand and giving it a squeeze. "We met at the funeral of her last husband."

"Then why did Thelma say Match?" asked Adolph

"We don't usually talk about this with strangers. It's easy to say Match, and people just accept that, without questions. Thelma's embarrassed that we met at her last husband's funeral. She thinks that sounds unseemly. I think it's romantic."

He continued, "I was at the funeral home for the wake of a friend of mine when I saw her across the hall at another wake. Randomly, we made eye contact. I wandered over and waited in the reception line. When I shook her hand, I could feel the sparks, the special chemistry between us. I slipped in beside her to talk to her and shook hands with everybody who came by, like she did. Everybody assumed I was a member of the family.

"That night I wrote a story inspired by her, a pornographic story. I gave it to her the next day at the funeral when I was standing close to her. It rained. I had an umbrella and shared it with her. I drove her home. She told me that reading that story while sitting beside me in the car gave her an orgasm. We've been together ever since."

"Well, Thelma, what about the rest?" asked Adolph, "What about the seven other men who have shared your life and your bed?"

"I married young. Fresh out of high school, I got a job as caregiver for an old man. He didn't think he needed help, but his kids insisted and paid. He was a widower. He had been married for sixty years. He had married his high school sweetheart and never touched another woman. I liked the man. I wanted to make him happy. So, over time, I got touchy-feely with him. We had our playful routines. I made good use of my hands, and then my mouth as well. He enjoyed it. I could make him happy with so little, and it was great fun to give him pleasure that he had never imagined he would feel again. But nothing would get a proper rise out of him. You know what I mean. Then I tried role play, making up stories to go with our caressing and cuddling. Once, in fantasy, I suggested that we get married. That was our first wooden moment, but it didn't stay up for long. He said that was because he couldn't delude himself into believing that it was real. Fantasy wasn't enough for him. I really liked the guy. Aside from the inaction of his equipment, he turned me on. I figured, what the hell? I married him. It was a private ceremony at his house. His kids hated me. They thought I was a predator, swooping in to marry the old guy for his money. I insisted, over his protest, that we do a prenup and that he draw up a new will with his kids as the only beneficiaries. Everything would go to his six kids and nothing to me.

"On the night of our wedding, he was ready, oh so ready. We went on a honeymoon cruise, the first cruise for both of us, and we rarely left our cabin. We did it three times a day on the slowest days. Our record was a dozen. Then we stopped counting.

"I was nineteen then. Now I'm over eighty. And, no, I won't tell you how much over eighty.

"When my first husband died, I married another eighty-year old. And then again and again. Each husband lasted five to ten years. Happy years. Except for one marriage that lasted fourteen and wasn't happy at all. I finally divorced that one, my only divorce. He's still kicking now at a hundred and three. From what I hear, he's playing Viagra games at The Village.

"Stan here is an eighty-year-old like the others. In my book, that's prime time. Aged to perfection. Only this time, my husband is younger than I am. I'm the older woman," She smiled and gave him a kiss.

Stan added, "I was a judge for twenty-five years. But the best judgment I ever made was marrying th," she replied and kissed him again, this time overtly inserting her tongue in his mouth.

"Bravo," exclaimed Adolph. "Now let's hear from the other couple." He nodded toward the pair sitting on the other side of the table, fit and trim thirty-somethings, in matching bright-red short-sleeved shirts, both with long brown hair, tied in ponytails. "What do you two have to say for yourselves and for our entertainment?"

"We're Jane and Randy, from Boston," Jane said before Randy had a chance to answer. "I used to be a welder," she said proudly. "When I graduated from Harvard, I got a job in the Quincy Shipyards. I learned the trade from my Dad. I was never interested in organized politics, but I wanted to raise the political awareness of workers at the shipyard, and I identified with the sexy welder lady in the movie *Flashdance*. When guys hit on me at bars, I enjoyed the reaction when I told them I was a Harvard grad and also a woman welder.

"Randy's an artist. Oils. Surrealistic. Good stuff. A hundred years from now he'll be discovered. For now, he works as a guard at the Museum of Fine Arts.

"I'm now a management consultant. I tell big companies how to get bigger. That's a far cry from welding and rabble-rousing in the shipyards. The arc of our lives isn't predictable. There's no telling where we'll end up.

"Randy doesn't need to work. He could focus on his art while I put the food on the table. But he wants to pull his weight, and he enjoys being in the presence of great art and watching the reactions of visitors who don't know the artists or the paintings and stare in fascination, without knowing why.

"And how did you meet? Was it love at first sight?" asked Adolph.

"You could call it that," she replied. "Or you could call it *love at first barf*."

Jane and Randy: Love at First Barf

Jane explained, "Back in my days as a welder, I first saw Randy at the buffet on the third evening of a two-week Caribbean cruise starting in Fort Lauderdale. Our eyes didn't meet. But I noticed that as soon as I looked away from him, he looked at me. Then when I looked back at him, he pretended to be interested in something at the other end of the food line.

"I was fortunate to find a seat near a window through which I could watch the sunset. He found a seat nearby, but he could have sat closer. There was even an empty place at my table-for-two. He sat facing in my direction, so while paying attention to his dinner or looking straight ahead, he could check me out through the corner of his eye. When I finished, I headed for the elevators to go down to the Piazza, where there would be dancing. He followed casually, as if without purpose, drifting back about twenty feet. When I stepped into an elevator, he raced forward and got in before the doors closed. He stayed close to the door, with his hands in his pockets. When the elevator stopped on Deck Five, he walked quickly straight ahead, apparently taking no notice of me. When I got to the Piazza, where the band was playing, he was leaning against a column and staring at me. He smiled, walked toward me, took my hand, and led me to the dance floor.

"Without saying a word, we danced to one song after another, fast and slow, disco to waltz. We didn't talk during the breaks, but stayed on the dance floor, hand in hand, waiting for the band to return. I felt a disturbance in my stomach. I thought it was butterflies, self-conscious nervousness. I had been attracted to and then disappointed by other men, time after time. I was afraid of emotional whiplash. Behind his smiles, I sensed that he, too, felt discomfort. Maybe he was as drawn to me as I was to him, and he, too, feared this would turn out to be a delusion. He, too, hesitated to put this moment to the test. It would be all too easy to slide into the familiar dating pattern, saying things that we had said time and again before, flirting, sharing anecdotes and life stories, filling the time until it felt socially acceptable for us to be alone together and see how far our emotional momentum would take us. With each dance, the tension mounted. I could see it in his face. And I suspected he could see it in mine. Then as we stepped toward one another in the cha cha, I lost control and vomited. A moment later, he did as well. All over one another. In the middle of the dance floor.

"The dancers around us scattered. The band stopped. Ship personnel took up positions around us to shield others from us. In a couple minutes, medical and security personnel had us in hand. My keycard, hanging from a lanyard around my neck indicated my room number. They escorted the two of us to my room, presuming that we were traveling together. There they took our temperatures, checked their pulses, and read us the riot act. There was no need to do testing. Norovirus was a common occurrence. That's a gastrointestinal ailment, a nuisance, not a danger. Most people recover completely without treatment. They said we should expect more vomiting and diarrhea for a day or two. We would continue to be contagious for three days after the symptoms ended. Over that time, we would be quarantined in our cabin. Meanwhile the whole ship would observe strict protocols designed to prevent this highly contagious illness from spreading. All surfaces throughout the ship would be cleaned frequently with disinfectant. Everyone entering the buffet would have to wash their hands with Purex. In the food lines, there would be no self-service. Ship personnel would plate all food. While under quarantine, we could not leave our cabin for any reason. We could order any food at any time from room service, at no charge. If we needed anything else, we could call our cabin steward.

"Gathering our personal information, they realized that we had separate cabins. Quickly, without thinking, I blurted out, 'We're together.' Randy smiled, nodded, and took my hand.

"Finally left alone, I started to talk, embarrassed to have been so forward as to suggest that we, complete strangers, share a cabin for the duration of the quarantine. He stopped me with a kiss

"That first night, with our stomachs on edge, we just cuddled. But by morning, all signs of our stomach ailments went away, and we began exploring the physical possibilities of our togetherness. We each admitted that we had been drawn to one another immediately. We suspected that our nervousness at the prospect of meeting one another had triggered the stomach upset. We probably didn't have norovirus. Nevertheless, we reported to the medical staff what they expected to hear, and we enjoyed our quarantine. It was like a honeymoon.

"When the cruise ended, we moved in together. Six months later we had a wedding with all the trimmings."

"Delightful! Congratulations!" exclaimed Adolph.

"Now you, Adolph." insisted Jane.

"Call me *Uncle Adolph*, please."

"Yes then, Uncle Adolph. It's your turn to tell a story. Tell us how you met Mae."

He flinched at the name of *Mae*. One moment he had been energetic, overflowing with contagious enthusiasm. The next he was deflated, like he had aged decades.

"Are you okay?" asked Jane.

He took a deep breath, sighed and admitted. "Your question brought her back to me, the image of her, how she looked thirty years ago. That's good, mind you. I should think about her. I don't want to forget her. She wouldn't want me to forget."

Adolph: Against the Odds

After another deep breath, Adolph plunged into his story, "I play the ponies, always have, always will. I'm a pro at it. I know the horses, the riders, the tracks, the weather and how that affects the horses. But I'm also a romantic. It's not all business to me. Once a month, I place a hundred dollar bet on a longshot, just for the thrill of it. And once I won big, very big.

"I was at Hialeah, near Miami, my favorite track by far. I had bet a hundred on a nag named Maybe, at odds of a hundred to one. Coming out of the gate, the favorite pulled up lame. I was standing pressed against the chain-link fence near the finish line. Coming into the stretch, Maybe was neck-and-neck with two other horses. I started shouting, "May! May! May! Go for it May!" And a lady standing beside me started shouting the same, grabbing hold of the top bar of the fence and doing chin-ups in her excitement.

"It was a photo finish among three horses. It took forever for them to decide the winner. The tension built. Not that I needed the money. My luck had been running good lately. But it feels great to win a longshot, like a gift of the gods. I wanted to feel that rush. And it came. Maybe won.

"The lady and I jumped up and down with glee. We hugged. Then we kissed. And we kept hugging one another after the burst of joy ended.

"She had bet two dollars, so she won two hundred. My hundred-dollar bet was worth ten thousand. Back then, thirty years ago, you could pay for a year at Yale with that kind of money, or you could buy a damn good car. That was serious money.

"We walked hand-in-hand to a cashier booth.

"We pooled our winnings and spent it together over the following months.

"Her name was Mable. Her friends called her Belle, but to me she was always Mae.

"May I unbutton this? May I kiss that? Every day was May Day."

Then Adolph turned to me, sitting to his left, "Now what about you, sir?"

Abe: Love at First Washcloth

I paused. I had enjoyed listening but would have preferred not to tell my own story. That was my business and no one else's. On the other hand, I would never see these strangers again, and they would soon forget what I said. Maybe talking about it could be therapeutic.

"My name's Abe. I'm a high-school English teacher, a would-be novelist. I've had one story and two poems published. An agent took on a novel of mine. She got a few nibbles. But when it didn't sell, she dropped it. I haven't been able to get another agent since."

"All hail the writer of fiction, the writer of wrongs," pronounced Adolph. "Do two writers make a wrong? How many wrongs does it take to make a ladder?"

I grinned. He was a performer. I couldn't help but be amused by his bad jokes, even when I was the butt of them. I began, "My wife, Babs, died suddenly five years ago, when she was forty-two and I was forty-five. We were married for twenty years."

"And how did you meet her, Abe?"

"She hit me with a wet washcloth."

Everyone laughed.

"Now what are the odds of that?" said Adolph. "Love at first washcloth."

I replied, "I'm reminded of a phrase that Harry used, 'The threads of fate come together.' In this case, there were three layers of coincidence that led to us meeting."

Beth interjected, "So, like Harry, you think that events magically unfold, outside the realm of probability, so lovers can meet. And that's how the human race perpetuates itself? By way of impossible coincidences?" She chuckled.

I tried to explain, "After the fact, events that are important to you feel like they were inevitable. All the pieces fell into place miraculously, and it's difficult to imagine how things could have worked out if those events hadn't occurred exactly when and how they did.

"On average, when you toss a coin, the probability of heads is fifty percent, regardless of the results of previous tosses. But you can't guess with certainty any single toss or any series of tosses, like heads, heads, tails, heads, tails. And the long chain of events that's your life feels inevitable because the odds against the occurrence of that particular series of coincidences are astronomical. Every moment of every life is unique and miraculous."

"Enough with the theory," Beth interrupted. "Tell us what she looked like."

"Babs had short black hair with perky turn-up curls at the end, framing a round face, with round cheeks, and a complexion so light you'd expect freckles. She didn't use makeup, not even lipstick, or she used it so well that she created the illusion that she didn't. She had a little-girl look of innocence and Christmas joy, even at the age of forty. But that, too, was an illusion. She knew that everything passes and that what matters to us is beyond our control. But she chose to wear a happy face, to enjoy the moment and help others to enjoy it as well."

"So why did she throw a washcloth at you?" Beth insisted.

"I was a grad student at Yale. It was the beginning of spring break. While I was walking along College Street, an old friend, Cal, happened to drive by. I hadn't seen him since graduation the year before."

"That's the coincidence?"

"That's the beginning. Cal was living in California, teaching high school in Watts, trying to make a difference in the inner city. He had just visited his girlfriend, his future wife. On his way back to the airport, he took a detour to drive through the campus, and savor memories. By chance, he saw me. He stopped. We talked for a few minutes. He had to keep going or he'd miss his plane. But first, he wanted to introduce me to an old friend of his who was at Albertus Magnus, a Catholic girls' college in New Haven. This was in the days before cellphones, so we ran across the street to a phone booth. He called her dorm room. No answer. He called again in case he had dialed the wrong number, and he let it ring maybe ten times. She answered. She had packed her car and was about to drive home for spring break, but her car wouldn't start, so she had returned to her room to call a garage for help. She heard the phone ringing when she was on the stairs, and she raced to get to it in time. Cal introduced us over the phone."

"So why the hell did she throw a wet washcloth at you?"

"She didn't. The girl Cal introduced me to was Nan. Babs was her best friend and roommate."

"You dated Babs' roommate?"

"Yes. Later, after spring break. The washcloth thing happened the first time I visited their dorm room."

"And what triggered the washcloth thing?" Beth pursued.

"Babs was annoyed that I had her friend's full attention, when she wanted to talk about a trip they were planning to Europe when school ended. It wasn't until a year after that that I realized that I was in love with Babs. But that first time I saw her was when I fell for her. The flash of anger in her eyes, the passion, the spunk. She was irresistible.""

Adolph laughed, "Yes, Abe, that was quite a coincidence."

"But that was just the first one."

"Well, what happened next?" he asked.

"It's what happened before that's incredible. If I hadn't known Cal, I wouldn't have met Nan and then I would never have met Babs. And it was extremely unlikely that I would ever have met Cal. That chain of events started back in junior high school in Plymouth, New Hampshire.

"My family moved to Plymouth from Baltimore. My Dad got the job of Dean of Instruction at the teachers' college. Plymouth was like the town in *Our Town*. Twenty-five hundred residents, far fewer than the passengers, much less the crew, on this ship. Everybody had a party phone line. To call out of town you needed to go through an operator. The town published a calendar every year with everybody's birthdate and anniversary. It cost fifty cents to be included.

In Baltimore I had been neither popular nor sociable. Now, suddenly, I was a celebrity, a newcomer in a town that rarely had newcomers. Before I had made friends with anyone, my seventh-grade class nominated me to run for vice president of the student council. My opponent, Judy, knew everyone. She was the daughter of a local preacher and had lived in Plymouth her whole life. She won by two votes."

"And where is this story going?" Beth prodded.

"Have patience, please. Soon after the election, my mother's Aunt Ethel died, and Mom and Dad drove down to Philadelphia for the funeral. They were gone for a week. During that time, I stayed at the preacher's house. There I got to know Judy and her brother Johnny. Judy and I got friendly enough to hold hands a couple times when nobody was looking.

"Then a week after my parents got back, the preacher was offered a job in Hartford, Connecticut. Two weeks after that, they moved. I corresponded with Judy and Johnny for years."

"So, Cal was a friend of Judy?" Beth guessed.

"No. He was a friend and classmate of Johnny, who was two years younger than me. Normally our paths would never have crossed. But I spent a year at school in England before I went to Yale. And Cal skipped his senior year of high school to go to Yale. So. we ended up in the same class despite my being two years older than him, and Johnny introduced us by letter."

"And that's it?" asked Beth.

"There's one more piece. My mom and dad had a hard time talking about death and preferred not to think about it. They never went to funerals. But Aunt Ethel had raised Mom, after her parents died back in 1932. Mom had to show up for Aunt Ethel.

"In other words, if my grandparents hadn't died in 1932, Aunt Ethel wouldn't have raised my mom, and she wouldn't have felt obliged to go to her funeral, and I wouldn't have stayed at the preacher's house, and I wouldn't have gotten to know Judy and Johnny before they left town, and I'd have never met Cal and never met Nan and never met Babs."

"And that's all true?" asked Beth.

"Yes, I changed the names, except for Babs, but it all happened just as I told it."

Harry grinned and added, "But facts don't make a story true."

"What do you mean by that?" I asked.

"The Russians have a word for the truth of mere facts—*pravda*. That's accidental truth. This happens, then that happens. But there's also essential truth, the kind of truth that can shape your life."

"Are you talking about religion?" I asked.

"Let me tell you a story that happened to my father, a story about the value of stories, how fiction can be more important than mere facts."

"Let's save that for tomorrow," suggested Adolph.

The dining room was empty. Rinaldo was hovering, politely, waiting for us to finish so he could go off duty. We had missed the show.

"That was a fine start today," Adolph declared. "Now, all of you, your assignment is to watch, to listen, to snoop, to speculate. Go on a scavenger hunt for stories, on the ship and on shore at Princess Cay, and come back here tomorrow at five fifteen, when the dining room opens and before it gets crowded. Ask for this table, number eighty-two. Together, we'll dine on stories, fresh stories, with whipped cream and chocolate sauce."

Day Two: Princess Cay, Bahamas

Authors aim for plausibility. *Truth is stranger than fiction* because authors don't write about life as it's actually lived, with its impossible coincidences. For them, a coincidence is only acceptable as an initial premise. The ending must feel inevitable based on the personalities of the characters and all that has come before. Authors believe that if they wrap up a story with a coincidence, the reader will feel cheated and manipulated.

Fortunately, the story tellers at our table were not professional writers, and the tales they told were not intended for publication. We were free to say what we pleased, with no such constraint.

On Day Two, everyone showed up on time, and we got the same table, with Rinaldo as server. Uncle Adolph was decked out as before in white suit and straw hat, as if this were a play and that his costume. Randy and Jane once again wore matching short-sleeved shirts— this time bright shimmery green. Beth had added blue highlights to her hair and wore a plaid vest and skirt with colors to match her hair. The attire of the rest of us didn't stand out. I remember their words, but not their clothes.

Thelma and Stan: Blow Job Bliss

Thelma announced proudly, "Stan and I won *The Newlywed Game*! Just like I said we would. Starting tomorrow, you'll be able to watch it in your cabins on Princess TV. We just celebrated on the balcony above where the tenders dock. I leaned over the railing, wearing a beach dress with nothing on underneath and Stan pleasured me from behind. Then we used the champagne we had won to toast the passengers on the roofs of the tenders below us. Stan did remarkably well in both the contest and our celebratory aftermath. "

"No problem there, my love" Stan added. "You make damn sure of that. She puts Viagra in my coffee every morning. It's a huge turn-on that she wants me that much. That would probably make me horny without the chemical boost."

We all laughed.

She caressed his cheek and looked him in the eye. Then she turned to the rest of us and explained, "Since Viagra came on the market, twenty years ago, all my husbands have wanted it. It's a matter of self-confidence, which is important to a man. Since I came on so strong, they doubted that they could keep up with my appetite. I told them all that I put Viagra in their coffee in the morning, and they all performed to the satisfaction of both of us. But all I put in their coffee was Splenda."

"Ah! True love," Adolph concluded. "How delicately and intricately truth and lies and love are entangled."

"Handwoven," added Beth.

"And woven with other parts as well," Stan confirmed.

"Yes," said Thelma, "*The Bible* says speaking in tongues is holy, and tongues can speak in many ways, even soundlessly. We were reminded of that today on the beach, after our celebration on the balcony. There we met another newlywed couple, at least as old as ourselves. Stan and I were floating on our backs, rising, and falling with the waves, enjoying the panorama of a mile-long beach, punctuated with breakwater rock formations, with our ship in the distance. We drifted near a couple we had never seen before, who were standing in waist-high water, and sharing a bottle of chianti that they passed back and forth, drinking straight from the bottle. They greeted us like long-lost friends. They had been in the live audience for our *Newlywed Game*. They had admired our performance. The gentleman—he never told us his name, and I was so focused on what he said that I forgot to ask him—he entertained us with his life story, unprompted, like he was itching to share it, as if he wished that he and his wife had taken part in the contest and had had a chance to shock the audience even more than we did. He claimed he had divorced his first wife, after fifty-two years, because she wouldn't give him a blow job. Yes, *blow job*. That's what he said to total strangers."

Then Thelma switched to a deep voice and gestured with her hands, imitating the man. "He said, 'In all that time, she never did it once. Then I met this fine lady.' He put his arms around her, pulling her close. 'She has the tongue of an angel,' he said. His wife drank the last drops of chianti, then smiled and took hold of the bottle with both hands. With her head back and the bottle held high, she put the mouth of the bottle in her mouth, like a sword swallower, or like a porn star doing deepthroat. We all cheered her on. Their uninhibited joy was a revelation and an inspiration. I'm sure we'll add some of that to our repertoire tonight."

"Indeed, we must," Stan agreed. "The Fountain of Youth was an illusion. But when two people, like us, can honestly tell one another what we want, and share our fantasies, that's the Fountain of Truth."

"The *hornucopia*," Adolph exclaimed. "To blow jobs!" he toasted, raising his glass of cranberry juice. The rest of us raised wine glasses to join him. "That's a fine appetizer to go with tonight's Surf and Turf. Now, Harry, you promised us a story about truth and fiction."

"Yes, the way fiction can be truer than facts."

"On with it, my lad."

Harry: The Bugle Boy

Harry began, "In the Second World War, my Uncle Don was a bugle boy in the infantry and about to be shipped to the front in Germany. The day before he was to leave, he got orders to go to OCS, Officer Candidate School. His company wound up in the Battle of the Bulge. They were all captured—safe and sound. Then the train taking them to prison camp was bombed by the Allies, and the guy who took his place as bugle boy was killed, the only casualty.

"When Don heard that story, it changed his life. The replacement bugle boy had died for him. Now it was his responsibility to live a life worth living, to do unto others, to follow the straight and narrow. He had been directionless. Now he felt he had a destiny. He had been chosen and saved. He owed it to that fellow soldier who died for him to do his best in every way he could. He became a teacher, then a principal, then a superintendent of schools. He stayed in the Army Reserves and rose to the rank of colonel. He married and had five kids and sent them to the best schools. He did his best to raise them to be upstanding citizens and mothers and fathers.

"Then, after he retired, at a veterans' reunion forty years after the war, he chanced upon someone from his old company, someone who was captured with the rest at the Battle of the Bulge. From him, Don learned that the story he had heard and that had shaped his life wasn't true. The bugle boy survived. He had recently died of a heart attack, but he came through the war unscathed.

"The facts didn't matter. Learning the truth was like adding a footnote to the story of Don's life. His life was shaped by a falsehood. But it was a good falsehood. And he felt fortunate that he had believed it and that hence had lived the life that he did."

Jane: Meter Maid Marion

"Let me go next," Jane volunteered. "There are many flavors of truth. I want to tell a story about an author falling in love. This is a true story not because it happened to me or to anyone I know. It's true because I can imagine it happening. It should happen. If it hasn't happened yet, it will happen sometime."

She began her tale, "Bill had writer's block. Day after day, he sat at his computer, opened Word, and stared at a blank screen, until his itchy mouse finger took him to Twitter where he could react to questions or witty observations and forget his deadline.

"He needed to clear his head and get ideas to flow as they always had before. He could easily lose himself online and another day would disappear. He turned his computer off and went for a walk, north up High Line, then cross-town to Fifth Avenue and up to Central Park. The whole way, he didn't have a single idea. He looked without seeing. He counted his steps. Two thousand steps per mile, he remembered. He lost count at six thousand, but continued walking, zombie-like.

"Three blocks south of the Met, he encountered a meter maid, in a freshly starched or brand-new uniform. Wide-eyed, she turned her head this way and that, scanning up and down the street, as if, for her, this was a new adventure, the start of a new life. He guessed this could be her first day on the job. This was now her domain, her beat, and she was proud of it.

"Twenty feet away, he stopped and stared. Physically, she was very attractive, but that wasn't what caught his attention. On this long walk, he had passed dozens of women who in a technical sense were more beautiful than she. But she had an aura of freshness and enthusiasm that was contagious. The cleft in her chin. Her green eyes. Her freckles. How would he describe her to someone else or in a story? He was good at dialogue and weak at descriptions. He needed a life writing class, like life drawing, with a woman like this posing naked for him to sketch in words.

"She was a meter maid, and he wanted to meet her. He had to write that down.

"He reached in his pocket. He had a Sharpie, but no paper. Whenever he went out, he carried a pocket-sized pad of paper in case he got ideas. But it had been so long since he last had an idea that he had forgotten the pad when he left his apartment.

"He felt this was, at last, the onset of a story. He needed to jot down what he was thinking before he lost the thread. His imagination was working again. He needed to record this scene right away and find out how far this idea could take him. But he had no paper.

"He couldn't return to his apartment. That would take too long and the distractions going there by foot, by cab, by subway, by any way at all, would kill the idea. If he looked for a store where he could buy paper, that too would kill the idea. *Meter Maid Marion*, he repeated over and over to himself.

"Then it occurred to him that he had cash in his wallet. Money was paper. He could write on money. It was worth it to sacrifice money to keep the inspiration alive. He ran to a bench across the street, on the sidewalk beside Central Park. He took a one-dollar bill out of his wallet and started writing on it with his Sharpie. When he had filled that with text on both sides, he took out another bill, then another, then another.

"That's when he realized that he wasn't alone. The meter maid who had triggered this wave of inspiration had followed him. She was standing in front of him, staring at him with a look of disbelief and concern.

"He looked up. Their eyes met. That gave him still more ideas. He opened his wallet again. Fortunately, he had a stack of ones. There was no telling how long this story might be, and he had to write this down immediately.

"Arms akimbo, with a look of authority, she addressed him. 'What do you think you're doing, sir?'

"'I'm writing a story,' he said, waving her off, not wanting to be interrupted.

"'You're writing on US currency, sir. You're defacing US currency. That's a crime. Do you realize that that's a crime?'

"He chuckled and kept writing.

"She pulled out her cellphone, did a quick search, and announced with authority, 'Violation of Title 18 Section 333 of the United States

Code. Punishable with a fine and/or imprisonment for up to six months or both.'

"'Interesting detail. Thank you. I'll work that in.'

"'On the contrary, sir. You have to stop. Immediately. I can't allow you to deface currency in the presence of, with the full awareness of an officer of the law.'

"'Great. Thanks again. *Deface. Officer of the law.* I appreciate your help.'

"Marion was new on the job, her first after graduating from college. To her, this was the start of a career in law enforcement. Starting at the very bottom, she would work her way up. But here was someone challenging her authority. If a supervisor were to chance upon her with someone blatantly breaking the law in her presence, she would be humiliated. What could she do? She couldn't handcuff him and arrest him. She didn't have handcuffs, and she had no more authority to arrest than an ordinary civilian did.

"She sat down on the bench beside him and buried her head in her hands. She took a deep breath and tried to put this into perspective. Was she making too much of this? Was she making a fool of herself?

"She picked up the stack of bills on the bench between them. If she was going to do anything about this, the money would be evidence.

"She started reading and did a doubletake. He was writing about her. He described her as *a vision in blue* in her brand-new uniform, on the sidewalk across from Central Park on Fifth Avenue. In the story, seeing her had triggered an uncontrollable urge to write about this moment and to use the only paper at hand, US currency. The story moved quickly from a physical description of her to a one-sided conversation as he tried to get her attention, walking in lock-step with her as she went about her rounds, until she finally agreed to a first date, the next day, Saturday. They met at the Met. Then they got together half a dozen times for walks in the park when she got off duty. They went to a couple of movies. They spent a night together at her place, then a night together at his place. She moved in with him. They married and had three boys and a cocker spaniel.

"This guy was totally whacky. Stalker at first sight. Probably dangerous.

"She should run for it.

"Then, as she was putting the stack of bills back down on the bench, slowly, carefully, so as not to draw his attention, he stopped abruptly. His wallet was empty. His look of despair moved her. Rather than leave, she pulled out her own wallet.

"'How many do you need?' she asked.

"'One more, just one more. For the title. Before I forget. Thank you. Thank you.'

"On it, in big capital letters, he wrote, *Meter Maid Marion*.

"She cringed. That was spooky.

"How did you know my name is Marion? My badge says, M. Rodriguez."

"It seemed natural. Meter Maid. Maid Marion. That must have been in the back of your head when you took the job."

"And your name?"

"Bill."

She laughed. "That must have been in the back of your head when you started writing on dollar bills."

"I guess we have that in common."

"What?"

"We trust our instincts."

"She grinned.

"They kissed.

"The wedding was six months later.

"They taped those bills to the walls of their apartment.

"They had three boys and a cocker spaniel."

Beth: A Special Romance

Beth held up her hand to volunteer and also to request a brief delay. She ate the last two shrimp on her plate, and then began, "This is a story I witnessed on another cruise, on the Star Princess, down the coast of Chile and around Cape Horn. This was a matter of mistaken assumptions. From observation, I guessed wrong. But later I learned the truth from the father.

"I saw an attractive young woman with a short man whose facial expression and gestures made me think he was mentally deficient. The woman treated him with understanding and compassion. She showed him the care and attention required by a child, but with the respect due to an equal. I presumed that she was the man's sister. Their loving relationship was remarkable. They were with an older man who I presumed was their father.

"Later I saw the woman and her brother playing in the indoor swimming pool, with their father watching from a nearby deckchair. I sat down next to the father and started to read a Grisham mystery from the ship's library. When I caught his eye, I mentioned how beautiful brotherly-sisterly love is. He looked at me in surprise, so I clarified. 'The couple in the pool. I've seen them with you before, and I guessed that they are brother and sister and that you are their father. Please pardon me if I guessed wrong.'

"They were from Acapulco. He told me that the man, who looked like a pre-teen, was his son, Alejandro. The woman, Beatriz, was his son's wife. He explained, 'My wife devoted herself to the welfare of Alejandro, our only child, who was born with Down's Syndrome. She loved him unconditionally. When she died, I was overwhelmed with all I needed to do for Alejandro. I hired one nurse after another at great expense. They carried out their duties as expected but treated Alejandro as if he were less than a person. They watched the clock, as if doing what they needed to do for him was a chore and they were anxious to get back to their own lives. Alejandro became morose, withdrawn. He asked for his mother and didn't understand why she was no longer around. He didn't know the meaning of death.

"'When he reached the age of twenty-one, I posted an ad on the Internet seeking someone willing to marry him and care for him for the rest of his life in exchange for room and board and a substantial stipend. I interviewed dozens of applicants before I met Beatriz. She was intelligent and compassionate. She was thirty and destitute through no fault of her own. She was an orphan. At fifteen, she had run off with a ne'er-do-well who had abandoned her far from the town of her birth. First, I hired her as Alejandro's nurse to see how they would get along. She took to Alejandro immediately, and he to her. She glowed in his presence and he in hers. When Beatriz and Alejandro married, I rejoiced that my son's well-being and happiness were now in the hands of a respectful and loving wife, not just a hireling.

"'As it turned out, all was not as it seemed. Beatriz was still in contact with Diego, her former lover. It was Diego who had convinced her to marry Alejandro, for the income, which she shared with him, but also for entry to a rich man's house. Diego intended that she would make it easy for him to steal from me, her father-in-law. She didn't hesitate to share her income with Diego and sometimes snuck out at night to spend time with him, but she balked at the idea of burglarizing her benefactor.

"'One night when I was away, Diego broke into our house, using what he had heard from Beatriz to guide him in finding valuables. She tried to stop him. He pushed her aside. Alejandro saw them struggling and thought that Beatriz was in danger. He flung himself at the intruder to defend her, fighting with abandon, thinking nothing of his own life in trying to save the one he loved. Diego fought back in self-defense. They grappled on the balcony, up against the railing. Diego called to Beatriz to help him fling the incensed Alejandro over the railing. Instead, she rushed to rescue Alejandro, and together they pushed Diego to his death.

"'Since then, the pair have been inseparable, devoted to one another.'"

Adolph: Hot Tamale

Adolph chimed in, "That calls to mind a hot tamale I saw in Fort Lauderdale after we had signed in and were waiting in the terminal for the ship to be cleared for boarding. This lady wasn't sweet and compassionate like Beatriz, but she was Mexican and unbelievably gorgeous. She had a pair of knockers the likes of which I had never seen, not even in Vegas, where the strippers are siliconed up. Flora was sixteen, and that rack was all natural. Her mother told me that when she saw how I stared at Flora, who was parading up and down the aisle, enjoying the attention she aroused, while her mother and the rest of us sat patiently waiting until we could go onboard. Her mother, Rosita, was proud of Flora's physical attributes, proud that at such a young age she could catch the eyes of men and make men do what she wanted.

"Rosita bragged, 'Already my Flora has won the man of her dreams. He's a young man still, but twice her age, who owns the Berlitz franchise for Mexico City. He's a wealthy man already, and he's ambitious, skillful, hard working. He will one day be far more wealthy.

"'Flora met Cesar when she applied for a summer job two years ago, when already her body had blossomed. When she came home, she told me, *Today I met the man I will marry.* She told me everything about him. His blue striped jacket, his tie with the emblem of Harvard, his gold tie clip, his diamond-studded cuff links. A wonder of a man. At first sight, he gave her the summer job, and a part-time job for the rest of the year. He didn't look her in the eye. He seemed shy and embarrassed in her presence. But he couldn't take his eyes off her chest. After she started working at the office in Plaza Polanco, he stopped by there two or three times a week, far more often than at other offices and far more often than he had before. She heard that from Maria, her workmate, who saw, they all saw, how he hovered near her work area and how he looked at her. She talked to me about him often, and she talked about him to her friends as well, getting advice on what to wear and how to wear it to show off her blessings.'

"Yes, her mother called her breasts *her blessings, a gift from God* that she should be grateful for and make good use of to win the man of her dreams. She went on, 'After a year had passed, he still hadn't taken her out on a date or kissed or even so much as tried *to cop a feel*, as you say in English. She was fifteen, a year older than she needed to be to marry with permission, and of course I would permit. With her body and the attention men paid to her, Flora thought she should have been married long ago. She wasn't getting any younger. She was ripe and ready.

"'She made friends with the man who serviced the elevator in her office building and learned what to press to make the elevator stop between floors, without an alarm going off. At the first opportunity, she got on the elevator alone with Cesar, hit up instead of down, then made the elevator stop. She pretended to lose her balance and stumbled up against him. He caught her. She put her arms around him, as if to catch her balance, and pushed his head down toward her *gifts of God*. He responded as a man should respond. With one hand, she unhooked her brassiere, making it easier for his hands and his mouth to do what he had long been lusting to do. That night he took her to dinner at Pujol, the most expensive restaurant in Mexico City. Two months later they were engaged. The ring cost more than the house I've lived in for twenty years. Now he's at Berlitz corporate headquarters in Princeton, New Jersey, for a week of meetings. He paid for our cruise. He'll return when we return, and the wedding will be the Sunday after, a church wedding with two hundred guests at the open-bar reception. He's paying for it all. Then we'll all live happily ever after.'"

I interrupted Adolph. "I saw her today. I'm sure it must have been Flora. There couldn't be two women on this ship built the way you describe her. I saw her walking along the beach at Princess Cay, in cut-off blue jeans and with a halter top that barely contained her overflowing youthfulness. All heads turned in her direction. She was like a movie star walking up the runway at a premiere. She clearly enjoyed the stir she was making. But she wasn't alone. She was walking about ten feet behind a member of the ship's crew. I believe he's the assistant cruise director. She was with him but pretending she wasn't."

"He was being discreet," added Rinaldo, our waiter. "It's forbidden to have relations with guests. He could lose his job."

"Well, apparently, he was willing to take that risk. The two of them walked past the swimmers and sunbathers, into a thicket beyond the beach."

"I saw them later," added Rinaldo, "on the last tender back, sitting on a bench beside one another, looking in opposite directions, but their hands played together at their sides."

"Ah, love, true love," Adolph intoned. "May her marriage be blessed. May her Berlitz man teach her to speak in tongues, all the tongues of the world, and enjoy all the gifts of God. And may she continue to spread the blessings of God's gifts to others as well."

Abe: Vertigo in Venice

"Well, Abe, it's your turn now. You're a professional, the only professional writer among us. Surely, you must have a story. "

I paused to finish my blueberry pie and to gather my thoughts, then I launched, "I mentioned that my wife, Babs, died suddenly five years ago. But I didn't mention that three years later, I met someone new on Match and we married. Yes, Match, Stan and Thelma. Some people actually do it that way, instead of in funeral homes. This is a tale from that time, a tale that I've tried to put into writing several times, but I've never succeeded. Perhaps tonight with these fine storytellers as an audience, it will take the shape it should. I call it *Vertigo in Venice*.

"It felt like vertigo, only I was at street level and at sea level. The street was the sea, the Grand Canal in front of the Santa Lucia Railway Station in Venice. I had a panic attack with no apparent cause. I felt like I was standing on the edge of an abyss. I had felt like this once before, when standing at the edge of the Grand Canyon. But this wasn't a physical abyss, rather the abyss of death and memory and regret and absence and emptiness.

"Babs wasn't there, and she should have been. This was a moment we should have shared but couldn't. Fate had failed us. This made no sense. I needed my life to be a story, but instead it was a series of disconnected scenes, still-shots that had no connection to one another. Run them together like frames in a film, and you'd see a blur—no motion, no direction, no point at all.

"The woman beside me was a complete stranger. We had married two days before in Connecticut, and this was our honeymoon. She could see my distress — anyone could see it. I don't know how I managed to stay on my feet. Hundreds of people were milling about, some rushing by, pulling suitcases on wheels, heading to the station to catch a train. Others were heading toward the water to catch a vaporetto water bus to get to a hotel or a business meeting or an elicit rendezvous. They all had to get somewhere quickly. They all had people they cared about who cared about them, and they needed to get to those loved ones as quickly as possible. But I had no such person. I was alone and empty, standing on the stairs outside the train station in Venice, beside my bride on our honeymoon.

"The scene in front of me included the Grand Canal, the eighteenth and nineteenth-century buildings across the water, an old church with its dome painted blue-green, gondoliers maneuvering for position, hoping to catch the eye of would-be passengers. The gondolas were picturesque, but too expensive for normal transportation—a luxury for tourists, like the horse-drawn carriages at Central Park in New York.

"That's the kind of thing I would tell Babs, or she would tell me, if we were there together.

"Stepping out of the modern train station into this scene was like stepping back in time, but it was also shockingly familiar, like I had been there before.

"Then I remembered that this scene appeared in *Indiana Jones and the Last Crusade*—a quiet moment near the beginning, before the frantic action started. It was like I was in that movie, which Babs and I had enjoyed together. I wished more than anything that I could be sharing this moment with her, holding her tight, and stepping over the brink of reality into a new world.

"She had been to Venice with her friend Nan soon after college, but I had never been there. We had promised one another that we would go together and stand at this very spot.

"But we hadn't. There were many things we had promised ourselves and each other that we never got around to. There would be time later. But there wasn't.

"We had lived in a cloud of possibilities, that gave texture and flavor to our otherwise ordinary lives. Dreams of what could be gave depth and substance to what was. But now that that cloud was gone, the world looked and felt flat and empty.

"The sun was shining brightly in Venice. It was probably a hundred degrees in the shade; but there was no shade within a hundred yards. Sweat was pouring down my face. No, that wasn't sweat. I was crying uncontrollably. I missed her so much. I missed the self I was with her. I missed the memories we had shared and the hopes for the future we had shared.

"My new wife, my honeymoon bride, yelled at me, 'What the hell is going on?'

"All I could say was, 'This scene, this very scene, on a day just like this, with a crowd like this, was in a movie I saw with Babs, and she would have loved to be here, to see this, and I so much want her to be here seeing this with me. Nothing makes sense.'

"'You're damned straight it doesn't make sense. How dare you wreck my honeymoon!'

"I should have known then that my second marriage wasn't going to work, that it couldn't work. But we kept trying for nearly two years.

"Babs would have loved to be on this cruise. Everything about this experience would be different if she were here. So why am I taking this cruise alone? There's a part of me that believes in miracles. Have you read the Joan Didion book *The Year of Miraculous Thinking*? For me, it's been five years now, hoping and almost expecting that something wonderful will happen to balance the horrible thing that happened, losing her. I made the mistake of thinking I had fallen in love again, and I had married again. Now that that second marriage is over, I go places and do things that Babs would have loved, as if part of me thinks that her spirit might be there. I don't go back to places we went to together. I don't even visit her grave. Rather, I do things and go to places I should have with her. I look for her not in the past, but in the future, in the dreams of the future that we shared."

Day Three: At Sea, Formal Night

Today, May 2020, in Connecticut, we have been under pandemic stay-at-home orders for two and a half months. Some areas are starting to re-open, but the contagion continues to spread.

Many of us, isolated physically, though connected virtually, are losing our subjective sense of time, with restless frequent-waking sleep and no externally imposed deadlines or expectations. Is there any reason to shave or to get dressed when no one will see you? Unreal rhythmless days and nights are morphing into an endless twilight.

How does this affect what we think of as coincidence, our notion of story, our idea of the likelihood of events?

What just happened to the world was unimaginable. The civilized world, the globally interconnected economy suddenly shut down and hundreds of millions of people are now in a socially distanced limbo which may or may not end, without timetable.

For me, for now, romance is out of the question. I meet no one. There are virtual online events and restless dreams. But the face-to-face interaction which is the essence of story simply doesn't happen.

The stories we told one another on that cruise two years ago feel eerily unreal in this new context. It's likely that cruising will be transformed, like professional sports teams playing with no in-person audience. It's hard to imagine that we will ever again gather around a dinner table, sitting shoulder-to-shoulder with strangers without masks, without gloves, without medically mandated precautions of any kind. Writing about that cruise, such a short time ago, is like writing an historical novel.

Recording these tales, how I long for the good old days, for the old normal. And how I envy the lucky people who have loving partners and are sequestered as couples. For them, this isolation could be a honeymoon, like the experience of Jane and Randy. But at what point does it cease to be a honeymoon? Two weeks? A month? Two months? With no end in sight?

Day Three of our cruise was a sea day, on our way from Princess Cay in the Bahamas to Saint Thomas in the American Virgin Islands. That meant that for dinner it was formal night.

I wore a dark suit, a light blue shirt, and a red tie. Adolph wore a top hat instead of his straw hat. Jane wore a brown pants suit and Randy a matching men's suit. Beth wore a blond wig and a white evening gown. Harry wore a black shirt and a white tie, with no jacket. Stan wore a tux, and Thelma donned the kind of dress an old maid would have worn in the nineteen thirties. It was black with a pattern of pink roses, but it had been reshaped with bare back, and a neckline that plunged dramatically, displaying the blessings God had bestowed upon her and that, with a little help from her garments, could still defy gravity.

Thelma: Deep Pockets

"I've got a hot one," Thelma announced. "I witnessed it myself, at the bar near the adult pool. Two old ladies. Well, they weren't as old as me, maybe sixty-something. They were wearing high heels, earrings, makeup, looking like they just stepped out of the hairdresser's. Yes, tonight's formal night, but this was the middle of the afternoon. They looked out of place. Country-clubish. Snooty.

"The one walks up to the other from behind, grabs her shoulder, spins her around on her barstool, and slaps her on the face.

"The victim rubs her cheek and stares back in disbelief.

"'You stay away from him! You hear?' says the attacker.

"'I have no idea what you're talking about.'

"'You know damn well. You chatted up his nurse last night. She probably gave you an earful about him. Painted a picture of him with deep pockets, money to burn. Just what you're looking for, I'm sure. Don't give me that innocent look. This morning you were all over him. You sent the nurse away, and you wheeled him everywhere, talking endlessly, making him laugh about this and that and nothing. I know your kind. I wasn't going to make a scene with him there to see and get upset. He has a weak heart. No upsets for him. Doctor's orders. I know damn well. I've been with him for eight years now. I've invested my time, some of my best years, and I'm not going to have you swoop in at the last minute and scoop him up.'

"'Are you talking about that sad and lonely old man I befriended out of the goodness of my heart?'

"'Out of the goodness of your pocketbook, I'll wager. Stay away from him, do you hear?'

"'That's outrageous. I'll do nothing of the kind.'

"'You damn well better!' the attacker screamed and slapped again.

"At that, the lady on the barstool stood and kicked her attacker in the shins, then slapped her on the cheek. A cloud of dust arose, the makeup was that thick. Then it was kicks and slaps this way and that, as everyone around stood and stared, dumbfounded at such behavior on a cruise ship. Then the original victim grabbed the other woman's hair, and it came off. It was a wig. The lady was bald. In a single motion, the other lady dropped the wig and kicked it. It landed in the pool. The bald lady screamed and ran, and her victim strolled away, calmly, as if nothing had happened.

"Ship security was there in a couple minutes, but no one could identify the combatants, who had been standing in a blind spot, where the security cameras couldn't capture their shenanigans. They were lucky. They won't be identified so they won't be kicked off the ship. But it made for an amusing show. They were two of a kind, I'd say. Both disgusting. Predators latching onto old men to get their money. Deep pockets, indeed."

"A memorable moment, I'm sure," said Adolph. "Would that I could have seen it with my own eyes. What do these ladies look like? In case I should be so fortunate as to see them myself?"

"The attacker, the bald one, was so dolled up and girdled up, it's hard to tell what she'd look like *au naturel* or *au* anything else. I wouldn't recognize her if we were in the same elevator. But the victim looked regal, aristocratic. Tall. Thin. Maybe sixty. Well-proportioned, but not top-heavy. A long face. A long thin neck. A sharp straight prominent nose. High cheek bones. Bright eyes. Long blond hair, not natural of course, given her age, but she doesn't spare a penny to take care of that hair. Few wrinkles, but probably not from Botox. She was self-controlled even when under attack. And she's probably been restrained for her whole life, not letting her feelings show on her face."

Beth: The Duke & Duchess of Coney Island

Beth volunteered to go next. "Jane, I loved your story yesterday, about the meter maid. They should put a plaque on that bench by the park. That reminded me of a story I heard years ago about another couple who met on a bench.

"Imagine two seventy-year-olds sitting on the same bench in Hyde Park in London, both reading the *Times*. The next day they both return to that same bench at the same time, each doing so deliberately, hoping to see the other again. This time, to their mutual surprise, they are both reading the same book *The Paris Affair* by Tatiana de Rosnay, a novel about discreet anonymous sexual affairs.

"Each is widowed and shy. Each assumes the other is married and is a woman or man of the world. They spend the entire afternoon together on the park bench, neither of them saying a word to the other.

"The next day they both return to the same bench at the same time. Only this time, rather than sit, the gentleman offers the lady his arm and they stroll around the Serpentine, the long winding lake in Hyde Park, near Kensington Palace, where Princess Diana once resided.

"They are dressed in everyday, inexpensive clothes. And each presumes that the other is ordinary, middle-class, retired.

"They enjoy the routine that they have slid into, the quiet companionship, and don't want to complicate matters by talking about their personal lives. Let well enough alone. Silently, they have discovered that they have that much in common. They value their own privacy, and they are content to grant the other the right of privacy as well.

"They each continue to bring that same book with them although both have finished reading it, and each knows that the other has finished. Each considers the book to be a discreet invitation to take their mute companionship to another level.

"One day, when they meet at their bench, instead of taking her arm, he dares to draw attention to his book and to hers. They smile, and he leads her past the Marble Arch, which used to be known as Tyburn, notorious as the site of public hangings. They walk along Bayswater

Road, past a pub that advertises that it was the last stop for criminals on their way to Tyburn. They go to a well-kept but non-descript middle-class hotel, where they check in as Eugene and Tatiana de Rosnay. She smiles at his creativity in the names he chose, the author of the book they shared and the reference to Pushkin's *Eugene Onegin* and the Tatiana with whom he had an affair. After they discreetly enjoy one another, they speak briefly to one another, using those names when addressing one another.

"They continue meeting daily, only now they go straight to the hotel rather than to the park. She insists on sharing the cost of the hotel room, not wanting it to be a burden on him, but also doing it in a way to imply that she is careful, just as careful and concerned about finances as he is.

"Then he tells her that he just won a tidy sum in the lottery, and he'd like to take her on a transatlantic cruise and a holiday in New York City.

"They sail on the Queen Mary II, an inside cabin on a low deck.

"They stay in a modest hotel in Yonkers and go downtown by train. She helps with the expenses.

"She has a delightful time, in a world unlike any she has experienced before.

"They extend their stay, then extend it again.

"In the summer, they rent a beach house near Coney Island.

"She wonders what he's telling his wife and how he can afford this.

"He wonders what she's telling her husband and how she can afford this.

"Then sitting on a beach chair, she on his lap, and both reading the same copy of the *London Times*, they see a news item about socialites who mysteriously dropped out of sight— the Duke of Wessex and the Duchess of Northumberland. They look each other in the eye and break out in chuckles. And that's where they stay, together, for the rest of their lives."

"That story is sweet," I noted. "But it's sad as well. It's sad that we age, and that time goes so fast.

"You get caught up in habit and day follows day, and year follows year as if nothing has changed," I continued. "Then you wake up one morning and realize that you look like your grandfather did when you were a child. And it's as if the change happened over night.

"Say you got married and your union survived your self-centered and ignorant youth, then your immersion in work, career and child rearing. Then maybe you're lucky, like I was, and you wake up one day and find yourself married to your best friend and lover, married to the perfect person, despite the fact that both of you are very different from the two people who were attracted to one another and got married decades before. But that's luck, dumb luck. You don't have any control over it.

"When my third child, Tom, was born with cleft lip and cleft palate, he needed a series of operations. The plastic surgeon who did the work explained that his job was to sculpt in four dimensions. He had to consider not just what the result would look like now, but what it would look like ten, twenty, fifty years later, after growth and aging and with the distorting effects of the scar tissue.

"If only we had the knowledge and the skill to craft relationships in four dimensions.

"That's one consolation of aging. When two older people meet, they don't need to try to guess the changes that will happen over decades. They can unabashedly live in the moment, like the Duke and Duchess of Coney Island. Love isn't just for the young. In fact, the old may have an advantage, which brings me to the story I'd like to tell tonight."

Abe: Love at Second Sight

I began, "Imagine a sixty-year-old man on a transatlantic flight. The plane is full. The seats are small, with little leg room. He's elbow-to-elbow with a stranger, a woman of comparable age, in the window-seat beside him.

"He's tired and lonely. He's a recent widower who went on a trip to Paris alone and saw nothing, met no one. He ate, slept, and wandered through the streets in a fog. Now he wants to sleep. The sooner the flight is over, the better. He's relieved that this woman beside him hasn't started a conversation.

"He drifts off and has a memory dream of when he was sixteen on a flight back from Paris, where he had spent the summer on a student exchange program. A girl his age was in the window-seat beside him.

"Short, maybe five-two or five-three, with jet black hair and a Botticelli face. She was wearing a bulky white sweater and a red and green plaid skirt. Her blue-green eyes were concentrating on *L'Étranger* by Camus, which she was reading in French without a dictionary. He presumed that she, like he, was returning home. He wondered if she, too, lived near Philadelphia, or if this was just the first leg of her journey. He wanted to strike up a conversation but didn't know how to start. It would have been easy when he first sat down, but he had let that moment pass, and he didn't want to get off to a bad start by interrupting her reading when she was deeply involved. He would wait. Eventually she would put the book down or a stewardess would offer food and drinks. He pulled a book out of his backpack, *Introduction à la Méthode de Léonardo da Vinci* by Paul Valéry. That should impress her if she noticed. He didn't take out his French-English dictionary, even though he would need it. He looked intently at the pages. He was so self-conscious that he couldn't make sense of the words on the page, but he turned the pages as if he were reading. Then he realized that he was turning the pages too fast to be credible. He hoped she hadn't noticed. He didn't want her to think he was a phony trying to impress her. He slowed down, turning pages at the same pace that she turned hers.

Otherwise, he sat stock still, maintaining what he imagined was a sophisticated, intelligent look, until he drifted off to sleep.

"When he woke up, the plane was dark, except for foot-level lights in the aisle. It took a while for him to orient himself, to remember that he was on a plane. Then he felt a strange sensation in his left hand. As his eyes adjusted to the dark, he realized that the girl's hand was resting on his. Apparently, she was asleep. Her book was open, upside down, draped across her lap. Her skirt was scrunched up, revealing her right thigh, nearly to her underpants. Her hand probably fell into his by accident when she fell asleep. Since her eyes were closed, he felt free to look at her closely. She was gorgeous. Her pouty lips, her cleft chin, the bit of hair above her nose between her eyebrows, every detail of her looks became to him an indicator of beauty, even though he had never thought of those features that way before. Her hand in his hand, their fingertips barely brushing, gave him an erotic sensation beyond anything he had experienced before, more intimate than a kiss, even a French kiss with his girlfriend back home. Dreamlike images passed through his mind—him talking with her and the two of them falling for one another and, despite all odds, finding ways to meet one another again, then their going to the same college, and later marrying, and having kids and grandkids. Their whole future life together flashed though his mind, and it was a wonderful life. And the first step would be to speak to her. But he was paralyzed.

"He didn't dare move his hand, much less speak. What would she think of him if she woke to find that this stranger beside her was holding her hand? And he didn't want to move his hand. He didn't want this intense sensation, this magic moment to end.

"He was hungry and thirsty. He had to urinate. But he couldn't move.

"He felt an electric tingle in his fingertips coming from her fingertips. She might be awake, just pretending to sleep. She might feel drawn to him, just as he was to her. This might be a moment of mutual ecstasy, more than just chance, the two of them fated to meet like this.

"Then, unprompted by his conscious mind, his hand squeezed her hand.

"He felt a shock of fear, mingled with hope. He would never have done that deliberately. This moment, this possible future life might now be over, ending in embarrassment and shame. How dare he take the hand of a girl he had never spoken to, a stranger on a plane? But having squeezed, he couldn't help but hope for a miracle, and the miracle happened. She squeezed back.

"He had to urinate badly, but he didn't dare break the contact, losing his only connection with her, his only hope.

"He studied her face. There was not the least sign of recognition or consciousness. She was probably dreaming, imagining that his hand was someone else's hand. By chance he had become a placeholder in her dream, a substitute for the person she wished she were with.

"He felt like an intruder. He didn't deserve her tender fingertip caresses, her gentle squeezes, her light sensory passion. But he welcomed any contact with her. If her feelings were already fixed on someone else, he had no chance with her, and this accidental contact with her was all he could hope for. He would savor it while he could and cherish this moment in his dreams for the rest of his life.

"Then he wakes up. Yes, he's on a plane. Yes, he remembers he's on his way home from Paris. But he's sixty, not sixteen.

"A woman's hand is in his hand, but it's not the hand of a teenage girl. It's the hand of a mature woman, about the same age he is.

"She's asleep, like the girl in the dream.

"Black hair with gray roots. Pouty lips. Cleft chin. A bit of hair between her brows.

"Her hand squeezes his hand, and he has an electric shock of recognition.

"'Hello,' she says. 'It's been ages since we did this. Maybe this time we'll get it right.'"

Adolph laughed, "Well done, Abe. I didn't see that coming. Now Jane and Randy, do you have a story to share, perhaps another love story?"

"Jane, let me take this," Randy volunteered. "I want to tell the one about *Love at Second Tattoo*."

Randy: Love at Second Tattoo

"Grace believed in soulmates. She believed there's life before life, as well as life after death, a *pre-heaven*. Souls mingle there before they're born, and some fall in love. Then, after birth, those who fell in love strive mightily to find their soulmates. Grace believed she had found hers in Jake.

"She and Jake planned to get married, but instead of an engagement ring, as a sign of the bond between them, at her prompting, they got matching tattoos—a monarch butterfly between the shoulder blades.

"But he cheated on her, and she broke up with him. That's what brought her to Pedro's tattoo shop, to get her tattoo removed.

"Pedro was shocked by her beauty. He had never met anyone like her. He was amazed and delighted that she was so easy to talk to, that he could talk at all, considering how much in awe of her he was. They swapped stories and puns for hours, while she lay on his tattooing table, her back exposed, and he worked on removing the tattoo, taking far longer than necessary and deliberately leaving a last piece undone, so she would have to come back the next day.

"She was out of his league. She was far better educated and upper middle class. He had never socialized with anyone like her before. But he was smitten, and he thought that she was attracted to him as well.

"He guessed that for her to take him seriously as a suitor, he would need something special, something other-worldly. She was into astrology and believed in fate and true love. She had thought that *Cheating Jake* was the one she was fated to spend the rest of her life with. And while his betrayal had nixed his chances with her, that mishap had not diminished her faith that somewhere she had a soulmate. Her real true love was still out there. She had to find him.

"Pedro was born with a birthmark on the back of his neck. It consisted of two interlocking circles. And Pedro was a calligrapher, as well as a tattoo artist. There wasn't much call for calligraphy these days. People preferred writing and drawing on skin instead of parchment. Tattoos were all the rage. But calligraphy could come in handy now.

"He composed a couple of paragraphs and wrote them in elaborate script on aged parchment. He would tell Grace that his mother got this document from a gypsy fortune teller. The text included an image of his birthmark and said that that was the sign by which he would recognize his one-and-only, the person he had fallen in love with in pre-heaven, the soulmate it was his task to find and love on Earth.

"While she was stretched out again on his tattooing table, he would use local anesthetic more broadly than the day before, including the back of her neck as well as between her shoulder blades. And distracting her with talk and with back rubs to ease her stress, he would give her a tattoo that matched his birthmark. When he brought that to her attention in a mirror, and showed her his own birthmark, she would think that they both had the same birthmark and hence were meant to be together.

"All went as planned. She was shocked to see the mark on her own neck and the same mark on his. She bought the story with far more enthusiasm than he could have hoped.

"Then she pulled out her iPhone and swiped through hundreds of family photos until she found one of herself as a baby, naked on a blanket, on her belly. And there on the back of her neck was that very birth mark. Her parents had had it removed, as an imperfection on their perfect child. And here, miraculously, the birthmark had reappeared when she found him, her true soulmate."

Adolph: Eternal Life

"My turn now," said Adolph. "Having heard about life before life, I want to talk about eternal life."

"This is a story my great-grandfather told me, and my grandfather, and my father as well. They told it differently, but it was the same basic story.

"I asked each of them why people grow old and die.

"Great-grandfather said that God gave Adam and Eve a choice. Either they could stay in the Garden of Eden and never age and live forever, or they could have children. And they chose having children.

"In his version of the story, Grandfather said that everyone is given that choice in pre-heaven before birth. And only one man of all the billions of people who have walked the Earth has ever chosen eternal life instead of children. And that man deeply regrets his choice as he lives on forever, alone.

"My father transposed the story to the future, and instead of pre-heaven before birth, in his version the choice came at the onset of adulthood and was given by a scientist. The scientist offered a treatment that made it so you wouldn't age, but with the side-effect that you couldn't have children. That was a difficult choice, but, with just one exception, everyone chose to age and have children.

"And that one person who chose the treatment later changed his mind and offered to pay a fortune to reverse it. The scientist accepted the payment. The reversal worked and that man had many children and grew old and was very happy.

"Unbeknownst to everyone but the scientist, there was no such treatment and never would be. Everyone must age and die, and nothing can change that. But the myth that scientist invented enriched the lives of everyone, making them think that they had a choice, and that their aging and dying was payment for the gift of life they gave to their children, out of love."

Day Four: St. Thomas, Virgin Islands

On Day Four, Adolph opened the proceedings by announcing that someone new would soon be joining us at the table. "Rinaldo, tomorrow we'll need a ninth chair."

"But that is most unusual, sir. That cannot be done."

"Have no fear, Rinaldo. I've already spoken to the maître d' and my money speaks eloquently. I'm sure that he'll give you instructions, or your immediate boss will. I wanted to give you a heads-up and beg the pardon of these other guests here assembled that we will be crowded at dinner for the rest of the cruise, because I have invited a lady to join us. You have heard tell of her under the moniker of *Deep Pockets*. I prefer to think of her as *Hot Pockets*. She prefers *Roxanne*, the name her parents bestowed on her, which, unwittingly is the name of the heroine of a novel by Daniel Defoe, a fortunate mistress in the days of King Charles II, when mistresses were well thought of and well compensated.

"You are all surprised, I'm sure. You can't imagine me, at my age and in my state of disrepair, attracting a lady friend. And you wonder why a classy lady would want to spend time with a bozo like me. I make her laugh. That's the key to the jewel box, right Stan?"

Stan and Thelma chuckled in reply.

"Well, for my tale today," Adolph offered, "I want to tell you about *Hot Pockets*, not *Deep Pockets*. We must do justice to *Lady Roxanne*."

Abe: Hot Pockets

"Yesterday morning, as I was reading a book in a deckchair on the Lido deck, along came this classy lady, stumbling, unsteady on her feet. At first, I thought she must be drunk, staggering drunk in the morning. *Scandalous*, as Beth would say. That's when I noticed the kids running from the kiddie pool, where the water was sloshing back and forth in waves, and a voice over the loudspeaker announced we were changing course to get away from the swells, but we should still dock at St. Thomas by 9:30. It was the sea that was making her stumble.

"That was the first time on this cruise that I had felt like we were at sea. This ship is like a floating city block. It's easy to forget that we're in the Caribbean and chugging along at ten to twenty knots. Of course, the lady was unsteady on her feet. Everyone was.

"She staggered to the deckchair next to mine, sat down, and stretched out. I went on with my reading. When I looked up again, she was gone.

"Last night, after dinner, I saw her again at a slot machine in the Casino, dropping tokens and pulling the handle time after time. She wasn't winning, just going through the motions, like it was comforting to do something mechanical to get her mind off something else. That's when it occurred to me that she matched Thelma's description of the victim in that cat fight she saw.

"She's a fine-looking lady. If you saw her hands and her hair, you'd figure she was about fifty. But the skin of her neck is loose, like an older woman. The neck is the first to go. And her neck is long and slim, and the scarf she wore wasn't enough to conceal it. In her younger days, she must have looked like that Egyptian princess Never Titty or Audrey Hepburn in *Roman Holiday*. I'd guess she's sixty-five or so, but still a very attractive lady. A bit flat topside. Nothing next to the rack on my Mae, God rest her soul. But this lady has a grace about her, a presence, they call it these days. The air of her, the togetherness of her drew my eye. And she was alone. She is one of the few unattached and unaccompanied ladies on this ship. I settled down at a machine nearby and watched her. She was so absorbed in throwing her money away that she didn't notice me staring.

"Here was a real lady with class and breeding, I would have thought, except for your story, Thelma. But given what you said, maybe her classy look was an act, a class act, part of the scam that was her shtik.

"Despite myself, I wished I had *deep pockets* because I'd be quite happy if she wanted to latch onto me. That's when I got this idea.

"There's no way she'd give me a second thought, any thought at all. Let's face it. I'm a fat old guy, not in her league, not in her social circle. But if she thought I had *deep pockets*, I could be a contender. I could get lucky, very lucky.

"I needed to make her think I was Daddy Warbucks, and I knew just the scam to pull that off. Scamming the scammer is a legitimate pursuit, in my book. Like they say, all's fair in love with a whore. And if she's picking up old guys for their money, like you said, Thelma, despite all her class, she was a whore.

"I had seen this scam performed in Atlantic City a year ago. I had all the stake I needed. I wasn't hurting for money. I had a lucky streak at the track last month, and I'd rather blow it on this lady than anyone or anything else. But to do it here and now, I'd need the help of a crew member, one with clout. And who should walk by but the assistant cruise director, Max from Australia, the one who latched onto the Mexican hot tamale I told you about. I knew him from three years ago on a different ship, same cruise line. Back then he was a rookie, assistant to the assistant to the assistant, whatever they call it in their chain of command, the lowest of the low. He owed me big time for getting him out of a jam he was in for fraternizing with an underage passenger on the library floor. Back then, it was after midnight. The library door was closed with the lights out. Max's boss opened the door and turned on the light switch, doing a routine check. I happened to be walking by and took in the story at a glance. I pushed the boss aside, rushed in, pushed Max aside, and started doing CPR and mouth-to-mouth on the young lady. To make a short story long, by the time I was done spinning an improvised tale, the young lady, now dubbed *my niece*, was thanking me and thanking Max for saving her life. She said an allergic reaction had made it hard for her to breathe. And the boss, who didn't want a scandal on his watch, grabbed this explanation and ran with it. He thanked Max for his clear thinking and quick action but didn't report the incident to his boss and didn't put Max in for a commendation, not wanting to draw attention to what had just happened, not wanting to know more and not wanting anyone else to know more.

"So, seeing Max last night, I went for a stroll with him and told him what I needed and why. He understood that I wasn't trying to get money from this lady. I just wanted to get into her pants. And me being me, I'd need quite a boost to have any hope of that.

"I needed a blackjack table and a dealer. I'd provide the chips, ones that I used for card games with friends, not at all like the chips used in the casino. The dealer would act like these chips were worth a hundred dollars each and that I was making big bets. The card play would be the real thing. I could win big or lose big, with all the drama as if it were real, but no money would change hands, except for generous tips to Max and the dealer. The lady would get the thrill of seeing big sums gambled and would see me as a wealthy gambler. I would play until I had lost every chip. She would feel sorry for me and comfort me. And, in her arms, I'd end up a big winner. My money was persuasive. He was ready to do it. But before I could pull the trigger, the lady disappeared.

"I went ashore on St. Thomas today but didn't venture far. I had been looking forward to taking a swim at Magens Beach. In my book, that's the finest beach in the world, even better than Princess Cay. But I was feeling down because I had missed my chance. I hadn't realized how much I was smitten by that lady, even though I hadn't so much as spoken to her. And I might never chance upon her again in the few days left of this cruise. I went back onboard and paced the halls, like a caged bear.

"Then I saw her again, sitting at the baby grand piano in the Crooner's Bar. The place was empty except for her. I don't know what she was playing. She didn't have sheet music in front of her. The piece was classy, probably classical. She played it soft and mournful, for herself and no one else. Sad it was. My eyes teared up seeing her there alone, sitting bolt-upright, unperturbable, and making music that was so soft and forlorn and vulnerable, like a message meant for the dead, in full knowledge that the dead would never hear it. I wish I could play like that and remember Mae while I was playing and know how happy she'd be to hear me playing like that and to know I was thinking of her.

"Lucky day of lucky days, Max walked by. The timing was perfect. The slot machines and the tables in the Casino were closed because we were in port. That would make it easier to pull this off.

"Max was all in. Since the Casino was empty, and there was only a skeleton crew on the ship, it would be easier to try my scam now than it would have been the night before. Max would play dealer, so I'd pay him double. I gave him my room card, and he ran to my room to get my chips. Meanwhile, I approached the fair lady, Roxanne, and gave her my spiel.

"I told her I was feeling lucky, very lucky. Such moments happen rarely, but when they do happen, you have to act on them. To turn your back on good fortune when it's offered to you is to jinx yourself for the rest of your life. She looked at me like I had six heads. I told her that life's a gamble, and if you don't gamble, you don't live. I told her I had this feeling, this premonition that she was the key to my luck. I needed her to stand by me and watch. Just half an hour. That was all I was asking for. The ship was going to open up one table in the Casino just for me because they knew I was a good customer, and they knew how important this was to me.

"She was confused by this ridiculous proposition. That was all the opening I needed. Before she could say no, I took her by the arm and led her to the Casino, talking the whole way, not giving her a chance to think or to reply. Max had set up a blackjack table. We were off and running.

"She saw me bet and lose what looked like tens of thousands of dollars, then win much of it back again, then lose again, up and down. I couldn't have written a better script.

"I played it cool, taking my losses in stride. I told her, 'What's money for but to enjoy yourself while you're losing it.'

"But she got emotionally involved, thinking so much was at risk. She cheered when I was ahead, and she begged me to stop when my stack of chips dwindled away.

"By the time I had lost it all, she was hugging me and comforting me. She really cared. It made no difference to her that now, to the best of her knowledge, I was totally broke. She hadn't been interested at first when I was a crazy stranger with lots of money. But when she thought I had lost everything, she was there for me, she cared about me. She wasn't looking for *deep pockets* after all. She was an empathetic, well-meaning, generous person. And she seemed to genuinely like me.

"Then I paid Max, in front of her, and explained to her what I had done and why. She laughed heartily, relieved, for me, that I hadn't lost a fortune and flattered that I had gone to such lengths to get her attention. She said she was impressed with my creativity. She said it was the best joke that anyone had ever played on her and that she needed a good laugh.

"That was when I invited her to join us at our table for dinner. She said she was committed for tonight but would come tomorrow. I think she wanted a chance to sort out what had just happened and to doll herself up before seeing me again.

"That's enough for now. You'll meet her tomorrow. I'm afraid I'm losing my objectivity as your ringmaster, becoming involved, hoping to get very involved with one of the subjects of our inquiry.

"Beth, please take the baton. Don't let me ramble on even more. Give us another love story."

Beth: Dance Instructor

Beth started, "It's easy to feel lonely on a cruise ship, lonelier than living alone, because you're forever reminded of your loneliness by the happy couples around you.

"It's easy to mistake relationships on a cruise ship. When you see two people on Fifth Avenue, you have no clue how they might be connected. They might have just met and be flirting. or they might be old friends reunited after many years, or they might be married to one another and miserable together but not wanting anyone to know that their marriage has failed. But when a couple goes on a cruise, the odds are great that they make one another happy, and sleep together, and enjoy one another. This might be their honeymoon or their second honeymoon or their fiftieth honeymoon. This is a special time for them, a time when they're freed from the distractions and responsibilities of everyday life, when they can delight in one another and connect and rediscover what it means to be in love.

"I'm sure when people see Harry and me together here, they think that we fit together like pieces of a jigsaw puzzle. We complete one another in our differences, in the way we walk together and talk together. We aren't two random people who happen to be with one another. We're a couple, a combined and inseparable entity. We aren't hydrogen and oxygen. We're water, with the unique properties of water, as if we were meant to be together from the moment we were born, or before that in a pre-heaven for souls like in Randy's tattoo story. Forces of nature brought us together so we could become the couple we were meant to be, that we had to be.

"When we saw this young couple dancing, Harry and I presumed they were together, really together, the way their bodies flowed together to the music. They didn't need to look at one another. They didn't need to talk to one another. They moved as one and enjoyed the movements and the presence of the beloved partner, now pressed close and now at arms-length, back and forth, but always, even when not touching, when each moved separately to the music, they were truly together.

"We figured she was maybe eighteen or twenty, maybe in college or maybe having left college to marry her partner, who was ten years older than she. He probably had a good job, doing well enough to afford this cruise and to have a house with a picket fence and a mortgage to force them to be financially stable and reliable. Eventually the house would be filled with a child or two or three and the couple would morph into a family.

"All of that was obvious to Harry and me watching them on the dance floor.

"Then, when the next song started, they left the floor, and he returned with another partner, a woman ten years older than he was, the same height as the first woman, the same general build, but more flesh around the middle. The same black hair, but short and shaped by a stylist, not long and flowing with the movements of her body, like the first dance partner.

"I guessed and Harry agreed that this was the young girl's mother, the young man's mother-in-law. He had politely invited her to dance, as he would have at his wedding, which, considering the age of his wife, had been recent, not more than a year ago. Maybe this was a first-anniversary cruise.

"But they danced too well together. If she was his mother-in-law, it was scandalous how tightly he held her and how delighted she seemed when she was close to him and how well they moved together, like they had danced together for years and slept together and had children together. Every characteristic of the relationship that one could presume from the dancing was beautiful and romantic when he was with the younger woman, but it was unsettling, almost disgusting if you believed this woman was his wife's mother, his Mrs. Robinson.

"The song ended. They left the dance floor. Then he came back with another woman, similar in build to the two others. At first, we guessed this might be the sister of the last one. Then when the flow of the waltz brought them near to us, we realized that she was older, old enough to be the mother of the last one and the grandmother of the first.

"Harry and I looked at one another in disbelief. The grandmother of the bride? Who brings along a grandmother on an anniversary cruise? Maybe it was a family thing, a very close family, and the father or the grandfather—no, not to be sexist, maybe the mother or the grandmother was wealthy and was generously paying for them all to be here and share in this family reunion.

"But they, too, danced too well together. The two previous pairings had seemed perfect from the harmony of their movements together. This one was beyond perfect. They executed difficult and elaborate moves, moves it would be almost impossible to imitate, and they did so with the greatest of ease. All eyes followed them. Couple after couple stopped in the middle of the floor to watch them, until they were the only couple dancing. When the song ended, the audience broke out in applause for them.

"They didn't stop there. They didn't leave the floor. They danced again and again. They danced waltz, fox trot, cha cha, rumba, merengue, tango. Their tango was exquisite and scandalous, the way she leaned back, her short hair nearly touching the floor, and she extended her foot, running it up the inside of his leg all the way to his crotch. This could have been a dance show in a cabaret, except she was older than sixty, and he was younger than thirty.

"We were mesmerized and dumbfounded.

"We came up with outlandish scenarios. He was making love with all three of them, both separately and as threesomes and as a foursome. He was a gigolo, and the grandmother was the one paying for him, and was sometimes sharing his services with her daughter and granddaughter. What else could you make of it?

"When the music ended and the band packed up, and the crowd dispersed, we spotted the four of them sitting at the International Cafe, enjoying a midnight snack. Our curiosity got the better of our manners. We walked up to them and congratulated them on their dance skills. I couldn't bring myself to ask about their relationship, but I did ask, 'How did you learn to dance that well? Have you been taking lessons for years?'

"'Yes, for years,' the grandmother replied. 'Antonio has been my dance instructor for ten years, and he has taught my daughter for, it must be, five years. And my granddaughter just started taking lessons from him. She learns quickly. She has talent. We all enjoy ballroom dancing and dancing with Antonio so much that I paid his way and pay him a salary besides, and I paid for his wife, as well, to come along on condition that he dance with us alone.'

"That's when we noticed the fourth lady, standing behind him, with her hands on his shoulders, smiling proudly."

"Bravo!" exclaimed Adolph. "We're off to a romantic start today," noted Adolph. "Jane and Randy, can you add a tale of love?"

Randy replied, "I have a tale of guitars as well as love."

"On with the show," Adolph cheered him on.

Jane and Randy: Dueling Guitars

"Alonzo was a professional guitar player on a cruise ship in the South Pacific. When the ship stopped at American Samoa, he went ashore with the passengers. He was jaded from having been on dozens of cruises all over the world. Only rarely did he go ashore at ports of call. Playing tourist was boring, rushing hither and thither to snap pictures that he would never look at. This time, walking down the hall on the Promenade Deck, he got caught in the surging crowd heading for the tenders, and, on impulse, he went with the flow. Once ashore, he disdainfully observed the passengers doing tourist things, and he amused himself girl-watching. There were scores of good-looking shop girls trying to catch the attention of tourists and lure them in to buy things they didn't need and gifts that their friends and relatives would soon ditch at yard sales.

"Then he heard guitar music, a tune he had never heard before. Sitting on the curb, near the town hall, in front of a combination tattoo and surf shop, a young girl in a faded cotton dress was strumming a guitar. She played with her eyes shut, switching from one haunting tune to another. It sounded like she was improvising, making it up as she went along. She was connected to her instrument, breathing the music, playing without thinking about playing.

"He waited for her to pause so he could engage her in conversation, but she played non-stop. He dropped coins in her hat, then dollar bills, then fives, then tens. But she took no notice of that. She was absorbed in her music. She didn't play for money. She played because that was who she was. She wouldn't decline money. She had put her hat out to solicit donations. But she didn't care about that. It was a beautiful day on a beautiful island, and she was a beautiful woman making beautiful music. Everything was in harmony.

"Alonzo ran back to the ship and got his guitar. He sat facing her on the curb on the other side of the narrow pedestrian street. He tried to mimic her, softly, so as not to break the spell she was under. He closed his eyes and listened and played until he got a feel for the emotion, the consciousness that was generating this music. When he could intuit the patterns and anticipate where she was going, he played louder, loud enough for her to hear. She opened her eyes and smiled, but continued playing, without saying a word. He started playing harmony to her melody and added improvisations, always returning to her melody.

"He had to go back to the ship for an afternoon rehearsal, and the ship would be leaving soon. He walked up to her. She stood and stopped playing. They kissed, with passion and hunger, oblivious of the tourists walking by. He told her, 'Come with me to the ship. If the cruise director hears you, he'll hire you, and we'll be together as we're destined to be.'

"She stared at him, conflicted. She couldn't decide.

"He left. He had to leave.

"Before the ship pulled away, he dashed ashore again. By jumping ship, he would lose his job and his chance to be hired again by this cruise line. In addition, he'd be blackballed so other cruise lines wouldn't hire him. But he simply had to. It wasn't a matter of choice. They were meant to be together.

"As he was racing to the curbside where she had played, she was racing to the ship.

"Security wouldn't let her up the gangway, so she started playing, and everyone turned to watch and listen. She said she needed to speak to the cruise director, and someone fetched him. Still playing, singing her words, she told him that she absolutely had to join this voyage. Entranced with her music and knowing that he had just lost his guitar player, he hired her on the spot.

"The ship left as Alonzo wandered the streets looking for her.

"A year later, she returned on the same ship and found him playing the guitar on the same curb.

"They've been together now for ten years. You can hear them tonight at ten o'clock in Club Six on the Fiesta Deck."

To everyone's surprise, Rinaldo interrupted to correct Randy, politely but firmly, talking about matters he knew well. "Yes, Alonzo and Marietta play well, very well. Even after a twelve-hour day, I go out of my way to listen to them. But the story you tell isn't realistic. It can't be true, at least the details about her being hired on the spot by the cruise director and Alonzo getting rehired after having been blackballed. Such things never happen in real life, only in story. Cruise lines don't work that way. Procedures and the chain of command must be followed. Hiring of entertainers goes through Corporate. To fill a temporary vacancy, they would call Corporate, and Corporate would fly out a replacement to join the ship at its next port of call. Your story is much more romantic than a true story would be. You tell it the way life should be, not the way it is."

"Excellent, Rinaldo," Adolph thanked him. "You add a dimension to our tale telling. Please feel free to join in and to tell stories of your own, if you can make time for that, while taking care of your duties at other tables."

"I'm not allowed to fraternize with passengers," objected Rinaldo. "Yes, I can and should be polite. A friendly word here and there is welcome and necessary. But I can't join in as if I was one of you and tell a whole story. It isn't done. It would be a black mark against me."

"Well, we would welcome your contributions," Adolph assured him, "if and when you feel inspired. If anyone gives you a hard time about it, you tell me, and I'll set things straight. Yes, I'll deal them a straight flush, and all will be right. Now, Abe, you in your widowed singularity, what can you say of love? What tale do you have for us?"

Abe: Pension Barbara, Vienna

"I told you how I met my late wife, Babs—the wet washcloth, her roommate Nan. The two of them backpacked through Europe soon after graduating from college. Their stay in Vienna was the highlight of the trip, which she recalled with warmth, but no detail other than mentions of tourist attractions, like the Lipizzaner Stallions. She wanted to return there with me, but we had responsibilities to juggle, our jobs and our kids, and it would be expensive. We put it off. We could do it next year. Then she died, suddenly, and there was no next year, there was no *we* anymore.

"When I was trying to get my bearings, on a whim, I splurged and travelled to Vienna alone. On my first day there, I walked through the downtown streets which were blocked off from traffic of cars and trucks, between the Opera and St. Stephen's Cathedral. I passed many pedestrians who, like me, carried the telltale tourist map of the city that is given out everywhere. Most pedestrians moved about in groups of half a dozen or more. But there were some alone like me, staring here and there, walking down the middle of the street, checking street signs, comparing them with the map, and moving on.

"Inside St. Stephen's, the gothic cathedral, which is the postcard symbol of the city, tourists crowded into the back area, fenced off from where worshippers worship. Beyond St. Stephen's, I chanced upon a narrow *gasse*, an alley for pedestrians.

"I realized that if Babs were with me, my experience of Vienna would have been very different. Alone, I had no connection to my surroundings and the other people. I wandered aimlessly and gazed at the buildings, struck more by the sameness of large cities than by any hint of difference. I shied away from shops. I had no use for dust-gathering knickknacks and mementos.

"Babs would have stopped at every shop to look at the window displays, and often she'd go inside and handle the merchandise and talk to the shopkeepers. Not that she would be looking for anything for herself. No, by nature, she was connected. When she travelled, she had a list of the people she had to bring things back for. I would grumble and complain about such useless activity, 'No one needs this stuff,' I would insist. 'No one will pay attention to gifts like that for more than a minute, and it'll take you hours to pick them out. Why do you waste our time in this city where we'll probably never return?'

"She would have smiled, and coaxed, and insinuated that I could expect friendly pleasures when we returned to the hotel if I'd just indulge her in this need of hers. And, in fact, the quest that seemed to me such a waste of time would have connected her to this city. It would have given her an excuse to look closely and to talk to the natives and to hear from them about other shops and other goods. Each purchase would have woven threads of connection between our moment together in Vienna and friends and relatives back home. This shop we were in would have been transformed. Instead of being a shop like every other shop, it would have become the place where she bought the stein for Tommy or the angel figurine for Ellie. She would have seen more and remembered more than I did. The experience would have become part of the fabric of her life. And the photos she would have taken, even if they were only photos of buildings and of the same buildings that appear on postcards, would have been connected with memories of people we met in shops and restaurants and *beer kellers*.

"Yes, Babs always considered eating and drinking a pleasure, and the choice of a place to eat or drink was another opportunity, another adventure, like shopping for gifts. She would have made this city her own. She would have eaten and drunk the essence of it. In contrast, I eat from necessity and rush to get to my next task, without knowing why I bother to do so.

"Here, alone in Vienna, I had no way to get to know this city. I had no social skills, no natural camaraderie, no inclination to buy gifts. I walked and stared and judged, disconnected.

"But I could imagine Babs here with Nan during the summer of 1971, just after she graduated from college and before we began going out together. Nan, like me, would probably have been detached, amused by Babs' enthusiasms, and not involved in them. But Nan would have been willing to linger in restaurants and *beer kellers*. The two of them would have been open to meeting unattached men, whether Austrians or tourists. The possibility of such adventures would have added flavor to each day's meanderings. Nan would probably have been more overtly on the lookout for such adventures, but the two of them would have sized up the desirability of one or another of the prospects they spotted in the distance. And sometimes they would've tried to catch the attention of a likely one, with a look and a smile, and then deliberately looking away.

"All the while, to Nan's annoyance, Babs would have shopped for token gifts and curiosities, always having a dozen more people on her list, and needing something for each of them from each country and each city they passed through.

"They would have seen the Lipizzaner stallions in training. They would have been tempted by theater or opera, but not speaking German, they would have shied away from live performances, not wanting to waste their limited cash on what probably would turn out to be a bore. But there was an endless variety of restaurants, and there were plenty of college-age tourist men, hoping for romance, just as they were. The two of them would have lingered here in Vienna, finding a low-cost *pension* in one of these alleyways not far from St. Stephen's, in the midst of all the charm of the old inner city.

"I was staying at the pricey Vienna Marriott and was tempted to move to a *pension*, a boarding house, the low-cost alternative to a hotel, favored by students. I wished I knew which one Babs had stayed at long ago. I was thinking, too, of the scenes John Irving wrote about his stay at a *pension* in Vienna, with gypsies and a trained bear and circus midgets. Similar scenes from several of his novels merged in my memory.

"There were very few *pensions* listed in my European travel book. It only devoted five pages to all of Vienna. But I suspected there must be many of them, so I broke away from my cynical detachment and began to ask, at restaurants, shops, and hotels, about nearby *pensions*. Having found one, I asked there for directions to another.

"To my surprise, I heard tell of one named *Pension Barbara*. The person who told me, on the square outside St. Stephen's, was a businessman from Canada. He had heard of it from a friend who had stayed there. He didn't remember exactly where it was. But he was sure it was near. He himself was staying at a plush hotel this time, on business, his company paying for it. But a friend of his, had come to Vienna when he was just out of college, and with several other friends, had stayed at *Pension Barbara* and had a great time.

"Asking for that *pension* in particular, I soon found it and checked in.

"I woke at dawn and saw on the stone wall across the alley a series of enormous paintings of a beautiful young girl who resembled college-age Babs. As the sun rose higher in the sky, the shadows shifted, and the images became darker and soon it was almost impossible to distinguish them from random patterns in the stone.

"I asked at the front desk, 'Who's the girl? And who did the paintings?'

"The clerk looked at me as if I were crazy, 'What paintings?'

"I insisted and took the clerk out to the street to look up, but nothing could be seen from there. I dragged the clerk up to my room to look out the window, but only the faintest hint, like a mirage, was distinguishable. The clerk laughed, like this was some game of finding artwork in the shapes of clouds or among the shadows the sun cast on mountain tops.

"I sought out the owner of the *pension*, and asked him about the name of the place, 'Why do you call it *Pension Barbara*? That doesn't sound Austrian.'

"The owner agreed. It was not a good name for attracting tourists. 'There is not enough Vienna in that name, yes,' he agreed. 'I should change the name. And now that you have awakened me to this reality, yes, I will indeed change it. I have a friend who knows consultants who are excellent at naming, which is essential in the tourist trade. Perhaps something with *Mozart* or *Edelweiss*. Best to leave that to the experts.'

"I insisted, 'But why this name in the first place?'

"'It was a whim of the previous owner, or so I heard. Something to do with an American tourist named *Barbara* who was just out of college, someone with a knack for getting people to open up and for bringing people together. She'd sit in the background. She was never at the center of the conversation, but when she wasn't there, there was no conversation at all, no gathering of young people. He didn't realize it at the time, but she was the reason he bought the place.

"The present owner explained, 'He was a young American, just out of college, with a high draft number. He didn't need to worry about Vietnam. He had a wealthy father and no reason to be one place rather than another. I don't remember his name. He chanced upon Vienna and upon this *pension* when Barbara and her friend, another American girl, were staying here.

"'Night after night the young people at the *pension* would assemble on the street, without anyone seeming to be the leader. They'd gather in a different *beer keller* every night. Then they'd return to the *pension* and, in the lobby by the fireplace, they'd talk and sing and enjoy doing nothing at all.

"'It was near Christmas and this wealthy American had planned to head home, but now he felt so good here that he wanted to stay forever. When he left, he went to plead with his father for the money to buy this magical *pension*. He talked passionately not about the physical structure or the business opportunity, but rather about the convivial spirit that brought him to life more than anything he'd ever experienced. He talked like someone in love, but it was as if he had just met himself, his true self. Here in this *pension*, he had become the person he wanted to be. These people, this time, this place made him feel alive as he never had before, made him fall in love with the self he never knew he could be.

"'His father gave him the money. He hurried back and bought the *pension*. His offer was outrageously generous, based as it was on emotion rather than business. He had only been gone for a couple days. It was still before Christmas. All the old gang was still here, except for one who had suddenly left for home.

"'Unaccountably, the atmosphere felt different. People said and did the same kinds of things as before. And there was the heightened excitement of the holiday and the celebration of his purchase. For several days, he offered free drinks and free accommodations, at random, wanting everyone to stay and preserve this moment. But the magic that had attracted him was gone. He felt empty and drank much heavier than he ever had before.

"'Then it dawned on him what was different. The American girl, the cute one with the black hair and green coat and the ridiculous floppy green hat was gone. He had hardly spoken to her. He couldn't remember a single exchange of dialogue involving her or about her. But wherever she was, everyone was animated. She didn't draw attention to herself, but rather to others, to their stories and their interests. Her attention was the spotlight that made others stand out and seem brilliant and amusing. And her spotlight never shone in her own direction.

"'He asked about her and learned that her name was *Barbara*. She had left for home before he got back with the money. And her friend Nan had moved on soon after, reportedly hitch-hiking to Spain. The page of the guest ledger with their registration had been ruined by beer that he himself had spilled in a drinking bout, so he had no record of their last names or home addresses. And Barbara had so rarely spoken of herself that all he could determine was that she came from Boston.

"'Now in the evening, when he returned from a *beer keller* with his new-found friends, this rich young American, proud owner of a *pension* in Vienna, sat in the faded blue easy chair in the corner where Barbara had always sat, and tried to see the room and his friends and himself through her eyes. He couldn't remember particular words she had said, just the rhythm, pulse, and tone of her voice, the way she began in the middle of a thought, saying something then backtracking. Sometimes she'd get annoyed that someone didn't understand the context of what she was saying, someone hadn't moved ahead from the current point in the conversation to where she had jumped to in her mind, and in backtracking and backfilling she gave new life and direction to everyone's thoughts and brought them together in a maze, where everyone's feelings and concerns seemed to matter more than her own.

"'He tried to reconstruct from memory her fingers — short, fleshy, surprisingly sensuous. He'd held them a few times at convivial moments when they all joined hands walking up the street and once or twice when they happened to dance together as a group.

"Her nose was flat on top and turned up, begging to be touched, begging for a friendly knuckle to brush against her upper lip and pass upward as if to relieve an itch between the nostrils, but really just to see the way she'd both back off and come forward at the same time, shying away from being touched, but wanting it as well.

"'She didn't flirt, overtly, like her friend did. She didn't push herself forward to be noticed, but she wanted to be wanted. She didn't expect to be singled out but was delighted to be included in the larger group. Although she probably didn't realize it, there was never any question about her being included. The group was only a group, only had life and purpose and direction from her unobtrusive caring presence among them. They were who they were because of her.

"'Before, the wealthy American had avoided going to the Historical Art Museum. It was too touristy. Now, he was at the door every morning when it opened. He went straight to the second floor where the paintings were, mainly Dutch and Flemish and Italian from the Renaissance. He studied the faces of the women carefully, and sketched many of them, not from appreciation of art, but rather striving to understand what made a face unique and memorable, finding a hint here and there of Barbara's face in the small portraits and in the vast panoramic biblical and mythical scenes.

"'He struck up conversations with art students who camped there day after day with their easels and palettes, making copies of these classic works. One such student, an Irish girl named Madeline, he hired to give him lessons in the evenings. He had talent at capturing the likeness of a person, a skill that was once considered at the heart of art and that now, thanks to photography, is considered merely a mechanical skill.

"'For practice and in hopes of perhaps seeing once again a flat turned-up nose or a green-blue eye that could sparkle in such a way that you forgot yourself and found yourself, he would set up an easel in Karntner Strasse and do five-minute pencil portraits of passersby. He accepted payment not because he needed it, but because it was expected of him.

"'None of the old gang remained at the *pension*. Even though he offered them a free place to stay. They all drifted on. There was nothing to hold them. Their drinking and joking had become hollow and repetitive. They sooner or later wanted to move on to fresh experiences or to head back to where old and new responsibilities awaited them.

"'Paying no attention to the business side of the *pension*—no publicity, no special effort to draw in customers from among the steady flow of young tourists in Vienna—he lost money month after month, and his father grew impatient with his requests for more cash to keep afloat.

"'Money worries began weighing on him, until Madeline, who he continued to see for lessons and who was now the only one left with whom he could share his obsession with Barbara, suggested that he do a mural on a grand scale. His neighbor across the alley, an accountant for a large corporation, who was rarely at home, was kind enough to indulge him, to let him use a large windowless cement-covered wall as his canvas.

"'That summer, a year and a half after Barbara had left, he immersed himself in this task. He built scaffolding by hand and mixed his own paints, all with the help and encouragement of Madeline.

"'By the end of September, the mural was nearly finished. It consisted of images of Barbara over and over again, large and small, sometimes only a head in a floppy green hat, sometimes full figure nude as he imagined her.

"'Crowds of tourists would gather to watch as he worked. Madeline would walk among the crowd with a hat, taking donations. Many of the tourists stayed at the *pension*, and Madeline would tell the legend of Barbara as they looked up at the scaffolding and the painting with spotlights shining on it, as he worked well into the night.

"'Then came the rain, slow but steady, day after day, more rain than we had had in Vienna in decades. He couldn't paint outside so he sat in the lobby with the guests, hearing Madeline spin tales about the mysterious Barbara who had this artist in her thrall.

"'He had mixed his paints well, with full knowledge of the underlying chemistry and the demands of the weather. But he had not counted on the persistence of the rain and the thinness of the cement he was painting on. Day after rainy day, the vast and glorious painting melted away, and the crowds at the pension melted way as well, leaving him with a strangely dirty wall and a losing business.

"'I never met the previous owner myself. I heard this tale from the washerwoman and the night clerk after I bought the place through a broker. At first, I thought I could reignite the mystique of the legend of Barbara, which had for a brief while made this place a Mecca for tourists. But Madeline, the spinner of the myth, had disappeared when the former owner did. I was unable to track her down. Perhaps they left together. I'd like to think they did.

"'All that remained was the name *Pension Barbara*, which, as you so accurately pointed out, doesn't ring true for Vienna. Yes, it should be *Mozart* or *Edelweiss*, or some other word clearly connected with Austria. My friend's consultant friend is sure to help with that. He's a professional with an international firm based in New York. Yes, he's sure to know how to make this place by name, brand, look and feel like the Vienna that tourists want to believe in and return to.'

"I stayed at *Pension Barbara* for two weeks. The time passed quickly. I was at peace with myself, sensing her presence, and realizing how lucky I had been to have met her, much less to have married her and lived with her for decades."

The table was quiet. It seemed the whole dining room was quiet, though that may have been me projecting my feelings on the world, needing a moment of silence to honor her memory and savor the echoes of our time together.

Then Stan broke the somber atmosphere, saying, "Let's end the evening on a light-hearted note. Here's a tale I call *Thanks for the Mammaries*.

Stan: Thanks for the Mammaries

"Bob was an advertising executive with a bright future ahead of him in sales of women's undergarments, especially brassieres. Starting in the art department, he had won praise and promotion for the beauty of the female forms he drew, especially the breasts. He drew small firm breasts, pert sexy breasts, and full round breasts. But above all, he was a master of large voluptuous breasts that seemed on the brink of bursting out of the narrow confines of bra, blouse or dress, the huge breasts of show girls and strippers.

"The other aspiring ad men he bypassed on his rapid rise to the executive ranks vented their envy by nicknaming him *Bob the Boob*. He countered by making breast jokes and expounding breast philosophies. He referred to the mammary protuberance as the *fountain of youth*. He claimed that it was the true symbol of the American nation—Mae West and the spirit of the Wild West, Marilyn Monroe and the American Dream. A huge burgeoning breast was the natural symbol of the forward-looking, striving vitality of the nation: its hopes, its aspirations.

"Bob was engaged to Sandra, a charming girl in all ways but one. Her breasts were small. He could call them *firm*, even *pert*. He could aesthetically appreciate their shape, and the way they went well with her shape. But they were not the voluminous, unaesthetic, bold fleshy swellings that had captured his imagination.

"He tried to be reasonable. There was no mistaking Sandra's beauty of person and form. But he craved that abundance, that super-abundance, that fleshly counterpart of the expansive vitality of America itself.

"Bob was convinced that with larger breasts Sandra would be more aggressive, more self-reliant, more vigorous, so much more the perfect wife for a young advertising executive with a bright future ahead of him.

"Being a true American, he did not simply resign himself to the situation. Rather, he did everything in his power to change it.

"After long months of study of the physio-bio-chemistry of the female breast, he developed a chemical that he believed could reactivate the growth cells of the breast and enable breasts that had been stunted to fill out to their natural abundant dimensions. Rather than insert foreign matter and artificially prop up the living tissue, this method allowed the breast to literally grow. When the experiments he performed on chimpanzees were uniformly successful, he told Sandra about it.

"Sandra was taken aback. She was, of course, aware that her breasts were below average in size. But since high school, she had learned to get along with her disability, had learned to choose the clothes that would accentuate her more positive features, and had eventually ceased to think about the size of her breasts. But from Bob's enthusiasm, Sandra could easily guess how much their size meant to him.

"For herself, she was content to remain as she was. She was suspicious of wonder-working drugs and chemicals. And, as he explained his method, she couldn't help but think of hybrid tomatoes and pumpkins growing to the size of houses. She wanted to laugh, but she didn't want to hurt his feelings. And she hoped that even if the experiment didn't succeed, and she was sure it wouldn't, the effort would cure him of his obsession, and they would be able to live together happily-ever-after.

"She let him give her the first injection.

"After a week, nothing noticeable had happened.

"After two weeks, Bob grew impatient and gave her another, much larger injection.

"A week more with no results, and he injected her again. She felt sure that when it didn't work this time, he would stop, and all would be well.

"For another week, nothing happened. But instead of accepting defeat, Bob became morose and buried himself in his basement laboratory, determined to perfect the treatment.

"Sandra was dismayed to hear that he hadn't perfected it before he tried it on her. She was still more dismayed at how little attention he paid to her now, and how surly he was when he did see her.

"She wanted to hate him, but she wound up hating herself, hating her small breasts. She lay in bed whole days at a time, staring at the ceiling or in the mirror across the room where she saw the two pitifully small lumps that lay so lifeless and blah on top of her ribs.

"Two months after the first injection, she thought she noticed a change. It scared her to think that she had become so obsessed that her eyes were playing tricks on her. She tried to pull herself together and go back to her normal pattern of life.

"A week later, a tape measure confirmed that her bust was a full inch larger.

"She didn't tell Bob.

"Another week passed, and she put on two more inches. She wasn't sure if the overall effect was becoming, but they were now statistically at least average, and, considered separately from the rest of her, they were attractive.

"At least Bob would be pleased. She was sure of that.

"She didn't mention what was happening the few times that Bob called.

"He was so busy with his advertising work and his experiments that a month passed without him seeing her.

"More time would have passed, but she got scared. Her breasts had continued to grow, slowly but steadily, and her bust was now thirty-six.

"The problem wasn't their size, but their shape. They had grown irregularly, grown in length without growing commensurately in width. They hung limply and painfully, for she wasn't used to supporting such weight. It was awkward for her to do anything but lie in bed, as she had done before, when her breasts had been so hatefully yet comfortably small.

"Sandra called Bob and, as calmly as she could, explained that his experiment had worked, but not as planned.

"He was ecstatic. Even when he saw her, he was ecstatic.

"With complete confidence, he gave her new injections near the base of her breasts.

"At first, his confidence seemed justified, as the breasts did, in fact, fill out and become full and round, and in succeeding weeks they grew still more to the huge voluptuous breasts of a show girl or stripper.

"Bob was in paradise, proud of his achievement. His dream was being fulfilled, the American Dream. He called Sandra his *butterfly* and lavished her with praise and love.

"She didn't know what to think. She was proud that he was proud, pleased that he was pleased. But she was uncertain that it was over, that her breasts had stopped growing.

"And they hadn't.

"Bob remained proud and enthusiastic as they rose to forty-one inches, forty-two, forty-three.

"When the tape indicated forty-four, he made a joke about *The Guinness Book of Records*.

"At forty-five, he joked about *Ripley's Believe It or Not*.

"At forty-six, he announced, more positively than before, that the growth had reached its peak.

"At forty-eight, he was clearly uneasy. He came up with excuses for why they shouldn't go out together in public.

"But the breasts continued to grow.

"At fifty-two, he called in specialists: doctors, biologists, sexologists, endocrinologists, biochemists, and physio-biochemists. He, at first, told them that this growth had just happened. But the forlorn look in Sandra's eyes made him break down and confess that he was guilty. It was his experiment. He explained in full what he had done.

"The doctors and scientists were amazed and congratulated him on his success and speculated on the scientific and market value of the discovery. They could offer no antidote, but rather stared in awe and even reverence at those huge breasts, bursting with vitality.

"At fifty-three, newsmen and photographers started besieging their apartment. Sandra was offered movie contracts by three major studios.

"By fifty-four, he was determined to stop this growth before it became hideous or even fatal. He called in world-famous plastic surgeons. But they stared in awe. When they said they could do nothing, Bob wasn't sure whether this was a limitation of science or if they couldn't bring themselves to touch with a knife what must have been the most voluptuous breasts the world had ever seen.

"They continued to grow. Sandra could no longer lie on her back because the weight on her chest was painful and made breathing difficult.

"They continued to grow. All of New York City followed their growth on the front page of the *Daily News* and then even of the *New York Times*.

"At sixty, a sketch of Sandra's breasts made the cover of *Time Magazine*. At sixty-five, her breasts overshadowed the Grand Tetons on the cover of *The New Yorker*.

"Bob and Sandra became the most famous couple in America. Sales of bras doubled, then tripled, and Bob's advertising company prospered in equal proportion. The whole nation had focused its attention on Sandra's bust.

"But the breasts continued to grow.

"A special platform had to be built to support them. A Las Vegas nightclub owner offered Sandra a million-dollar contract just to lie supine on his stage.

"Bob turned down that offer and all the movie contracts. He also turned down an offer of a vice presidency at his advertising company and quit his job. He spent all his days sitting by Sandra, tending to her needs, and, with her, staring in awe at the ever-growing, ever-swelling breasts.

"After a couple months, the media lost interest.

"It was always the same story. The breasts were always growing, and they were always the largest breasts the world had ever seen.

"But six months later those same breasts once again forced themselves on the consciousness of New Yorkers and Americans.

"They burst through the walls of the apartment...

"Then the walls of the building...

"Then the walls of the neighboring building.

"They were growing now at an alarming rate. You could see them swell like balloons, all the while maintaining their perfect voluptuous shape.

"Bob was first interviewed, then apprehended by police. He laughed hysterically but refused to say a word.

"The newspapers concluded that he had gone mad and had given the breasts a new and even more powerful set of injections.

"He was detained at Bellevue for observation.

"Sandra the person seemed to have disappeared. No one could see anything but those twin mounds of perfectly proportioned flesh.

"But while the newspapers speculated, the breasts kept growing: a foot an hour, a yard an hour, a yard in half an hour, ten minutes, a single minute.

"Soon all of Madison Avenue was in ruins. But no one dared raise a hand against the breasts.

"A billionaire had his skyscraper levelled by wrecking machines before the breasts reached it, for fear that they might be bruised in the effort by themselves. But he need not have worried. Nothing could stop them.

"Soon all of Manhattan was in ruins.

"Philosophers in Paris speculated on the meaning of the event: the dynamic relationship between quantity and quality, the transformation of subject to object, passive to active, the *pour soi* to *en soi*.

"Artists in Chicago greeted the breasts as living pop art.

"Southern Baptists claimed the end of the world was at hand.

"Women's rights groups hailed the beginning of the end of the exploitation of women. Thousands gathered in the Boston Common carrying *Breast Power* signs.

"Students at Berkeley went on strike to express their solidarity with the breasts.

"Students from Columbia marched in the wake of the breasts, singing *We shall overcome*.

"Harlem residents chanted, *Grow, baby, grow*, as their homes were levelled.

"A House subcommittee was formed to investigate the matter.

"And still the breasts continued to grow.

"Northern New Jersey was levelled. The normally conservative citizenry stared in dumbstruck awe at the power and magnificence of those mountains of voluptuous flesh.

"Blacks and Puerto Ricans, the poor and the young sang and danced and chanted and bared their breasts in solidarity with this natural force that was rising up in their midst and levelling the nation.

"Church-going old ladies were seen bowing down and praying to the breasts.

"Foreign tourists and pilgrims began arriving in droves.

"The sale of brassieres reached critically low levels as bras were burned in bonfires across the nation.

"Finally, a group of businessmen decided that the situation was getting out of control. Congress was too slow to act, and the Department of Defense dared not use force against the symbol of motherhood, apple pie, Hollywood, Madison Avenue, and the American Way. They flew to India seeking a solution.

"Within weeks, just as the breasts were levelling both New Haven and Philadelphia and brassiere sales had dropped to zero, an Indian Brahman designed and built a huge brassiere. A fleet of B-52's airlifted the bra from India and dropped it on the mighty breasts.

"Silence fell upon the crowd, upon the millions of refugees, upon the millions of demonstrators. The steady advance had lasted for nearly two months. Many were cold and hungry. Many were hoarse with cheering and chanting. No one moved. No one spoke. All watched anxiously as the breasts strove to burst out of the bra, watched, in the words of a French philosopher who had come to America to experience the advance of this extraordinary revolutionary movement, *the battle of form and matter*.

"When, after three days, the bra was still intact, people began to accept the fact that the breasts had been contained, that they would grow no more.

"The revolution came to a stand-still. It had lost its impetus, its vital driving force.

"Millions were homeless. The industrial and commercial capital of the world was buried beneath these extraordinary mammary mountains. The slow work of relocating and rebuilding began.

"Eventually, the nation returned to normalcy. *The Peaks of Progress* became part of the landscape, an American monument and tourist attraction."

Day Five: St. Martin

At a very early age we learn to recognize subtle facial signals, to make good guesses, interpreting what others are thinking and feeling. That's the closest we come to mindreading. In the old normal, facial language was far richer and more precise than spoken language or body language. Actors, especially screen actors, were masters at it. My dad was an actor in his retirement years, fulfilling a life-long dream. When he had a stroke and could no longer talk, his face remained expressive. He could make known his wants and feelings and could make friends and build relationships with just his facial expressions.

Now, during the pandemic, with everyone wearing masks, it's as if everyone had at the same moment lost that ability. Social distancing was forced upon us as a medical necessity. But the wearing of masks, a means of slowing the spread of the contagion, has distanced us mentally and emotionally.

These aren't the eye-level masks of a Lone Ranger. Rather they are medical masks, that resemble bandit masks covering mouth and chin. That limitation will force us to become even more expressive with our eyes to make up for what we miss when everything below the eyes is covered.

In the future, I expect that to appear in public without masks will be as unacceptable as public nudity. Virus-protecting masks will be available with an image of your own face or any other image you might want, like custom-made T-shirts, with photos, cartoons, slogans, advertisements. We'll need to learn new ways of detecting lies and building trust than by facial expression. It will be easier for those who grow up in the *new normal*, than for us who have the habits of a lifetime to overcome.

When we swapped stories on the Regal Princess, we had no inkling that we would soon face such challenges.

On Day Five, Roxanne arrived after the others had placed their orders and settled in. Adolph, wearing no hat and his white suit looking freshly pressed, repeatedly checked his watch, and looked toward the dining room entrance. She arrived, standing straight and tall, but walking slowly, like in a ceremonial procession. She wore a light blue pants suit. Her short blond hair looked like it had just been blown out by a professional. Rinaldo led her to the table and pushed in her chair. She didn't need to see the menu. She had checked it online. She ordered broiled lobster tail and king prawns, with a glass of Chardonnay.

She announced, "Adolph told me about your dinner talks, your sharing of stories. He warned me that I should be prepared to say something. So, I went off by myself on St.-Martin, rented a beach chair, and stared at the horizon, thinking about things I didn't want to think about, but should have. This could be therapeutic for me. So please pardon me for talking about myself, rather than inventing a story, for talking truth, rather than fiction."

Roxanne: Deep Throat

"I think I have cancer, but I haven't dared to check with my doctor for the results of the biopsy. He doesn't know I'm on this cruise. He has the number for my landline, not my cell. I haven't checked the voicemail on the landline. And he doesn't have my email address.

"Adolph told me that you know me as *Deep Pockets*, and why. Well, you should call me *Deep Throat* instead. The cancer that I may have, that I probably have, is throat cancer.

"My father had throat cancer. They operated. The operation was successful. They removed all the cancer. But the operation weakened the muscles of his throat, and he lost the ability to control them. He couldn't swallow. They could force-feed him through a tube down his throat to his stomach, but that was only temporary.

"Seeing him struggle at the end and knowing it wasn't cancer or heart disease that was killing him, but rather that he couldn't swallow, made me wonder if speech might be a secondary rather than a primary evolutionary development.

"Making noises with the throat may exercise muscles needed for swallowing. It's possible that the ability and desire to make sounds through the throat evolved because strong throat muscles are necessary for eating and drinking. And once the ability to generate a wide range of sounds had evolved, that capability could be used for communication, which further improved survivability.

"In the beginning was the need to eat and drink. The Word came later.

"At the end, Dad couldn't talk, but he could write. They put him on morphine to ease the pain, to let him die in peace. The hospice people were there for that and for me, to help me cope with the reality and inevitability of death.

"He passed out. We thought he was gone. Then two minutes later his eyes popped open, he reached for paper and pen and wrote: 'You mean I have to do this all over again?' Then he dropped the pen, shut his eyes, and was gone. I wasn't sure what he meant. Did he have to live his life over again? Or did he have to come back reincarnated in another body?

"I cried non-stop for a week, through the wake and the funeral and beyond. My daughter, Janine, stayed with me and forced me to eat and drink and lie down so I might sleep. My throat was sore, maybe from the non-stop crying and maybe psychosomatically, in sympathy with Dad and his throat cancer. Janine insisted that I see a doctor. I went to the same one who had diagnosed Dad. He saw the rawness and the swelling in my throat but needed a biopsy to determine if it was cancerous. I had the biopsy last Thursday. I booked this cruise as soon as I got home. It was a great last-minute deal. I didn't tell Janine or the doctor or anyone. I don't want anyone to tell me the results of the biopsy.

"I've been a bit scattered, and I've been inclined to befriend frail old men who remind me of my father. Enough. I thank Adolph for inviting me here and you all for welcoming me. It's time for me to be with people again, to return to the world of the living, for as long as I can."

After a pregnant pause, Adolph then asked, "So who gets to follow this tale of *Deep Throat*?"

"I've got one I'd like to tell," Randy volunteered.

Randy: Time-Shared Love

"You've all probably seen the band-leader singer Miguel. He does hip-grinding Elvis-imitations while breathing heavily into his microphone, like giving it a blow job. He sings all styles. He's a musical chameleon. Now he sounds like Chubby Checker, now like Frank Sinatra. He has a routine where he sings both parts of a duet, and if you shut your eyes you could swear it was Nat King Cole singing with his daughter Natalie. He walks through the crowd and around the tables, microphone in hand, and when he comes to a lady alone, no matter how old, no matter how young, he takes her hand, leads her to the dance floor and dances with her, his hips and hands and voice sending bolts of sexuality in her direction, to the delight of his partner and of the crowd.

"Well, he has a seventy-year-old groupie. Though he never dances with her, and she's the only unaccompanied lady he doesn't dance with, his eyes go to hers and hers to his, no matter who he's dancing with. Every night she sits at the same table, two tables away from the band, alone, slowly sipping a glass of white wine.

"Jane and I asked around. He's about forty, young enough to be her son. And she's a widow, who follows him, taking one cruise after the other on whatever ship he's on. He has a wife and twelve kids in Barbados, and she knows it. That's a fixed and unchangeable part of their relationship. Half the year he spends with his wife, and half he spends singing on cruise ships and sleeping with his seventy-year-old groupie.

"They're discreet in public, never walking together, never eating together, never going ashore together. But she sits at that same table every night from seven until midnight while he performs. She doesn't even talk with him during breaks. Then when the band packs up at midnight, she returns to her cabin, and soon thereafter he joins her there."

Rinaldo interrupted. "Please don't talk about this if there are officers around or the cruise director or the assistant cruise director. It's common knowledge that the two of them have a thing together, but if it were too obvious, if they were to flaunt it, if guests spoke too openly and loudly about them, management would be forced to take action. I know him. He's a friend. I don't want him to be hurt."

"Of course," said Randy. "I'll be careful. I wouldn't want to risk this sweet deal he's got. Working on a cruise ship must be the best gig in the world."

Rinaldo chuckled. "For us waiters and stewards and kitchen help and deck hands, it's not all that great, and the musicians don't have it much better. The hours they perform are shorter than the hours we work. But they practice on their own time, and they're given other duties, and they're always on call if the cruise director needs them. As for the rest of us, imagine what it's like working ten to fourteen hours a day, seven days a week, and going for months without a day off."

"What about the laws regulating work conditions?" asked Randy. "Surely those apply here."

Rinaldo chuckled. "This is an American company we work for. But the ship is registered in Bermuda. That means Bermuda work laws apply. And no one's around to enforce them. And no one's foolish enough to make a stink about it and lose his job."

"But you get free room and board."

"Our pay, with tips, amounts to about twelve hundred dollars per month. Do the math. Figure twelve hours a day, seven days a week. That's eight-four hours a week. About three hundred forty hours a month. Twelve hundred dollars amounts to less than four dollars an hour. No coffee breaks. No cigarette breaks. No breaks at all. Yes, for someone like me from Manila, any job is better than no job. And if I can keep up this pace for a couple years, and if I spend no money, I could go home with fourteen thousand dollars in the bank. Where I come from, that's serious money. But who can go two years without spending a penny? A beer on this ship costs four dollars. And when you're making about forty-eight dollars a day, a few beers cuts into that fast, and when you work the hours we work, you need something to keep you going."

"But if nothing else, you get to see the world," Randy insisted. "There's no other job where you'd get an opportunity like that."

"Yes, we sail all over the world, but we see nothing. We go everywhere, but it's like going nowhere. But don't tell anyone that I said this. As bad as it is, it's all I've got. And Miguel too, don't spread rumors about him."

"Understood. He's got a sweet deal with that groupie," said Randy. "No reason to wreck that for him."

"I don't know how sweet that is. It's not as clear and simple as you think. But that's the life he has chosen, and he should have a right to it."

"And what's not simple? Two ladies, like a time-share: half here and half there. And both seem to know it, and neither faults him for it."

"Two ladies, yes. But not the two that you think, or that this lady thinks. He's not married."

"You mean he never married the lady in Barbados, after siring twelve kids with her?"

"There is no lady in Barbados. No kids in Barbados. But there's another American lady, like this one, a widow. He juggles them, like a time-share, as you say. Half his time with the one, and half with the other; and neither knows that the other exists. Both think he spends the rest of his time with a wife in Barbados."

Jane raised her hand and interrupted, "It's my turn now."

Jane: Modern Bundling

She began, "After years of unsuccessful dating, Diane consulted a dating coach. 'I'm thirty-five,' she explained. 'My biological clock is ticking. I always presumed that I would have children, just as I presumed that I would find and marry the man of my dreams. I'm beautiful, brilliant, and well-educated. Men have always swarmed to me. Of course, the man I wanted would want me.

"'But, ironically, my looks turned out to be a curse. It was easy to meet and attract men, but not the right man. My suitors were all good looking and shallow, and they expected me to be shallow as well. Time after time, the chemistry was right, but after an enjoyable session in bed, we had nothing to say to one another. Time after time, I found myself nearly engaged to someone I didn't want to talk to, much less spend the rest of my life with. Some of them were really good in bed. But a vibrator is better, far better, and without the baggage. They were boring, totally boring. Thank God, I didn't marry any of them. So here I am, thirty-five, single, and childless.'

"'Have you tried online dating?" asked Cara, the coach.

"'Of course. I belong to Match. But there it's the same thing all over again, the same empty flirtatious conversations, some of which lead to dancing the horizontal mambo in bed. But that's just friction, and I want the real thing. I want a man who opens me up totally, who helps me become the person I can be and should be.

"'I'm a professor, a tenured professor of English at Yale. I've written books about romantic love as portrayed in nineteenth-century novels. But I don't have a clue how to find a man I can love. I don't have a clue what love is. I've never experienced it.'

"Then Cara asked, 'And how do you present yourself on Match?'

"'With photos, of course. Two dozen photos of me in different outfits and settings and activities. That's what men want. That's how they shop for women. I'm contacted by dozens of men every day. Some of them are very persistent. Some of them have very attractive photos.'

"'But what do you say about yourself in your profile?'

"'Damned little. The basic facts. All they want is photos. That's how to meet men, lots of men, with photos.'

"'But clearly, you don't want to meet lots of men. You want to meet *the* man. You should present yourself in a way that filters out those who are likely to be losers.'

"'You're more of a romantic than I am.'

"'Seriously. You're a scholar. You're aware that romantic love is a relatively recent concept. Up until a couple hundred years ago, and in some communities far more recently, marriages were arranged by parents or agents of parents.'

"'Do you expect me to go to a matchmaker?'

"'No. I expect you to be creative. When you blindly follow the current trends in dating and mating, you wind up meeting men you don't want to be with.'

"'Well, what the hell should I do? Tell me something practical, something actionable. That's why I'm here.'

"'Let's talk this out. Yes, talk. What's the longest you've ever talked to a man nonstop— just talk, no activity involved, no other people in a social group, just talk one-on-one?'

"'Maybe an hour, maybe a little more.'

"'And after an initial meeting, you either dumped them or let them advance on a track that led to bed, right? And on that track, there was little occasion for further talk, right?'

"'That's about the size of it.'

"'You'd have been better off in seventeenth-century England.'

"'You mean saddled with whoever my parents picked for me?'

"'I mean *bundling*. You know what *bundling* is?'

"'Of course. Not everyone did it, but it was common. A suitor was invited to spend the night in bed with a woman he might want to marry. It was a special bed with a board separating the two of them, and they were both fully clothed. But they could talk freely and get to know one another. It was a test drive. The parents picked eligible candidates, and the couple got a sample of what married life together might be like. But what's your point?'

"'Do it. Bundle. Do the modern equivalent of that.'

"'What do you mean?'

"'First, change your Match profile. Take down all those attractive photos of you. Replace them with one photo that makes you look your worst. Then write a profile that sets a challenge. For instance, you could say that you'll only meet face-to-face with someone you can have a phone conversation with for six hours straight and still be itching to talk longer.'

"'But no one would respond to a profile like that.'

"'Exactly. But if someone did, and if you did connect that intimately with him in a first phone conversation, that could be the one you're looking for.'

"'But what if it turns out that he's homely or even ugly?'

"'Would that matter if you connected to that degree? And remember, he's buying into this while thinking that you look as bad as your worst photo.'

"'But that's counter to all the popular wisdom. You should strive to look your best, to put your best foot forward when meeting someone, especially an eligible man. First impressions are important. People judge you based on your looks.'

"'And thanks to that popular wisdom, you, a beautiful, brilliant woman, are single and childless at thirty-five.'

"'I can't believe that anyone would contact me if I displayed a photo like that and proposed an absurd challenge like that.'

"'You're a grown woman. There's no reason you should wait for men to contact you. Scan the profiles. Go through hundreds of them. Take this seriously. Pay little attention to the photos. Look for well-written and intriguing summaries. Contact them and see if they get back to you. Then set up phone calls and see if one of them can meet the challenge. You can't do any worse than you've been doing the traditional way. And maybe this will work. Win or lose, it could be fun.'

"For a month, Diane looked at three dozen profiles a day, for a total of more than a thousand. From those, she picked ten to contact, none of whom replied to her. As she was picking up her cellphone to call Cara and vent, she saw on her screen that someone new had just looked at her profile. She checked his profile. One photo. Ordinary. Forgettable. Very forgettable. But his profile intrigued her.

"The profile read, 'Would you buy this used car? This used car has high mileage but is a self-starter, with low maintenance. It has a little rust around the edges, but it's reliable. It will take you anywhere you want to go. And it's special. It comes with a personalized ignition system. You can turn it on easily, but no one else can. Take it for a test drive. It will make you smile.

"'I am attracted to women with natural beauty, who are intelligent, self-aware, confident, who are comfortable with who they are, without pretense.

"'I'm down-to-earth, very casual, and prefer to be with a woman who is the same. I keep in shape—going to the gym. I prefer home-cooked food, and I'm used to cooking myself. I'm unselfconscious, direct, and candid. What you see is what you get.'

"She sent him a message, 'Want to talk?'

"He replied immediately, giving her his number."

"This was a longshot, but what the hell? She called him. His name was Rich, so when he answered, she asked, 'Are you filthy rich?'

"He replied, 'No. I shower every day.'

"A would-be author, he was unpublished, but serious about his writing. He had saved up from his job, as a technical writer for a computer company, to give himself a sabbatical, a year of doing nothing but write, hoping to finish a novel he'd been pecking away at for years. It was a collection of stories shared over dinner by passengers on a Caribbean cruise.

"They chattered away. She mentioned things she hadn't thought about for years. And she came up with new ideas about Jane Austen and George Eliot that she could and should include in articles. She started taking notes not of what he was saying, but rather of what she was thinking and saying.

"She admitted, 'I enjoy talking to you. But that challenge I put in my profile is silly. We should forget about that. There's no way we could talk like this for six hours or more.'

"He laughed. 'We passed that two hours ago.'

"She checked the clock. He was right.

"They agreed to meet on Saturday, in Milford, in the parking lot at Walnut Street Beach. She told him she'd be driving a red BMW, and she'd wear a summery red dress. He told her that he'd be driving a twelve-year-old purple Dodge Caravan, and he'd be wearing a straw hat so she'd be sure to recognize him.

"Hearing that, she nearly hung up, but bit her lip and closed with a cheery, 'See you soon.'

"When she pulled into the parking lot, he was standing beside his car. He staggered when he saw her step out. That couldn't be the woman in the Match photo. This woman looked like Nicole Kidman in her prime. But she was waving at him. That was her.

"She too felt wobbly-legged. That had to be him. No one else would drive an old purple Dodge Caravan and wear a straw hat. But this guy looked like Robert Redford in his prime, the days of *The Sting* and *Butch Cassidy*. Like her, he must have deliberately posted an unflattering photo.

"They've been married now for ten years. They have three boys and a cocker spaniel, just like the writer and the meter maid in my other story."

"Really?" asked Abe.

"You're the one who said that life is full of impossible coincidences." Jane smiled.

Beth noted, "That story makes me realize how difficult it must have been to be a mother in the days when parents decided who their daughter would marry. And it must be difficult today as well when a mother has no control whatsoever over her daughter's choice. I guess I should consider myself lucky that, because of the cancer, I'll never have a daughter."

Harry gave her a hug. She rested her head on his shoulder, then she launched into a story. "I'll call this one *Smothering*. This is what I imagine it could be like to be the mother of a teenage girl, remembering how difficult I was at that age."

Beth: Smothering

"Imagine a teenager. Her name is Laura. She's fifteen. She's your daughter. You love her. You're protective toward her. You always have been. But now, she bristles when you correct her.

"One day you ask her, 'What's wrong?'

"'Nothing.'

"'It's not nothing. I can hear it in your voice. I can see it in your face.'

"'What I don't say, I don't mean.'

"'But I'm your mother. I have mothers' intuition. I can tell when you're upset. I'm just being nice to you.'

"'Sometimes you're too nice.'

"You laugh. How can anyone be *too nice*. Nice is nice. Good is good. Maybe we should look *too nice* up on Google.

"'Google schmoogle.'

"'Please tell me what's wrong.'

"'Good God ...'

"'Don't use that language to your mother.'

"'I feel smothered.'

"You laugh again. *'Smothered*. Isn't that a bit extreme? I correct you sometimes. I've always done that. That's what a mother's supposed to do. That's one way a mother expresses her love.'

"'This isn't about me. It's about you. You treat me like a child.'

"'But you are a child.'

"'I'm not a six-year-old. I'm a woman. I'm young, but I'm a woman. I have my own tastes, my own wishes. And I want to have my own life. I need to do things—some things, not all things —my own way. Okay, I slip up sometimes on matters of hygiene or social grace. But most of these corrections of yours are about the *how* rather than the *what*.'

"'What are you talking about? There's a right way and a wrong way to do everything—'

"'Cut it please. Everything has to be your way.'

"'Not at all.

"'You're so controlling. You have no idea how what you say and the way you say it affects me.'

"'Me *controlling*? Give me examples. Please write down examples. I'm glad that you spoke up. That's a grownup thing to do. We need to work this out like adults. Write it all down in three columns. In the left column list instances that have happened over the last month. In the middle column list what you think about it. In the right column list what you and I together should do to deal with that issue.'

"'You're doing it again.'

"'What?'

"'*Controlling*. That's the very thing that drives me nuts.'

"'*Nuts*? What a strange word to use. That's so extreme. I bet that most of the things that bother you are minor, and when you write them down, you'll realize that. Often it's good to make a list of the things that bother you.'

"'You're belittling me. Over and over again, the things you say and the way you say them diminish me, make me feel small, make me feel like a child.'

"'You're being silly. Make the list, dear. You'll feel better and I'll feel better too, because that will make me feel closer to you. And feeling close to you is a reward of motherhood. That matters so much to me. And some day when you're a mother, you'll know what I mean. You'll realize that all these little things are an expression of my love.'

"'Jesus.'

"'*Jesus*? Don't you *Jesus* me. Don't speak to your mother that way. I won't put up with disrespect. Go to your room, young lady. Now. And don't come out until you're ready to apologize.'

"Shaking her head, waving her arms out and back to her sides over and over again, Laura stomps off to her room.

"An hour passes. Two hours.

"Surely she should have come to her senses by now.

"You knock on her door—no answer.

"You try the doorknob. It's locked.

"You fetch scissors and pry the lock open. You've known how to do this for years but didn't want her to know that you know. You understand that teenagers need a sense of privacy. So, you let her have the illusion that with a twist of a button she could have her own space, she could turn her room into her castle.

"She's gone. The window is open.

"You have a tremor of anxiety, then smile. Teenagers will be teenagers. It's natural. Sooner or later, she would want to run away. She's acting out. She's probably hiding in the back yard. Before long, she'll crawl back through that window. She'll be lying in her bed by morning. But, just to be sure, you look everywhere for her. If you didn't make a fuss about it, she'd have taken offense at that. Teenagers will take offense at anything. They're still kids at heart, much as they enjoy playing at being grownups.

"Laura can write that list tomorrow. Yes, the list is important. Open communication between a mother and a teenage daughter is important. You remember an article you read online about that subject. You'll point Laura to that article. Better still, you'll read it aloud to her. Better still, you'll force her read it aloud. You congratulate yourself. It's a good thing you know your daughter so well."

"Aha," Adolph laughed. "Love between generations. That may be even more of a challenge than romantic love."

All: The Next Generation and the Need for Fiction

"It's not easy raising a teenage daughter, or a teenage son either," I agreed.

"Methinks thou speakest with the voice of experience," said Adolph

"I've been through it three times. They're all grown and gone now. In no time, they'll have to deal with their own teenagers."

"Ah, the good old *generation gap*—echoes from fifty years ago. I used to laugh every time I heard that expression," said Adolph. "It reminds me of the phrase *God is our Heavenly Father*. Of course we don't understand God, and He doesn't understand us. That's the generation gap writ large."

I continued, "When I talk about teenagers, I'm also talking from my experience as a teacher. Seeing the next generation's lack of ambition, their lack of attention to detail, their simply not caring about academic matters, I'm concerned about the future of mankind. Today's high school and college students seek immediate gratification and are incapable of the sustained effort it takes to accomplish anything worth accomplishing."

Harry interrupted, "I beg to differ. Today's teenagers are concerned about the future of mankind, so concerned that they don't dare think about it. Like Thelma said on Day One: 'Life's short. Eat dessert first.' Tech makes it possible to get instant gratification—from videogames to online porn. Tech isn't the source of the problem. Tech provides ways to cope, ways to enjoy life when you have no belief system to motivate you to discipline, patience, and hard work. Previous generations had structured belief systems forced on them by their parents. Today's teenagers try to create their own belief systems from the wreckage of the past, or they try to avoid the *big questions* and enjoy what they can while they can.

"Environmentalists lament that the world as we know it won't last much longer. Today's teenagers have felt that threat their entire lives, without any hope of salvation. It's not surprising that they opt for carpe

123

diem like Thelma, rather than planning for a future that they believe will never come.

"A student who believed that it was possible to make the world a better place, to be part of the combined efforts of humanity, would have good reason to study hard and pay attention to detail. But a student who believes that the world is going to hell and there's nothing anyone can do about it, is going to eat, drink, and be merry. That's the crux of the problem. Real education requires faith in the future of mankind."

"It's not just teenagers," added Randy. "I made the mistake of telling my eight-year-old niece, as a trivial fact, that there are twice as many people in the world today as there were when I was her age. She broke out in tears because she concluded that there won't be enough food. She didn't need facts about global warming and ecology. She didn't need any science at all. Her inner Malthus saw the obvious consequences of over-population."

"I wouldn't worry about over-population," Stan objected. "I lament the demise of written pornography. That could have been a second profession for me, a way to earn after I retired from the bench. I had looked forward to that and the attendant notoriety. Now free video porn streaming over the Internet has made written porn obsolete. But that Internet porn is so compelling, so effective that it may save the world from over-population.

"Japan's ahead of the U. S. on that score. They already have reduced marriage rates and reduced birth rates. I see the development of video porn as a self-regulating mechanism built into our DNA. When tech reaches the point where artificial sex trumps the real thing, people don't put as much effort into mating. Why go through all the heartache and the expense, all the time and money it takes to get laid, when you can masturbate to your heart's content, for free, whenever you want? That's what students are up to. That's why they don't have time or inclination for study. But in the long run, that's for the good of mankind, avoiding the disasters of over-population. Rather than investing in birth control and sex education in third world countries, the U.N. should expand access to high-speed Internet and let pornography lower the birthrate."

"Pick your poison," I added. "Nuclear war, environmental collapse, or over-population. The disaster *du jour*. When my Dad was a kid, schools had duck-and-cover nuclear drills. They had to kneel under their desks and cover the backs of their heads with their hands, as if that was going to protect them from a nuclear blast, much less the fallout. Today's generation is the third generation in a row to grow up facing an imminent threat of human extinction. So how can we help today's teenagers believe that there will be a future? And they need to believe it, or mankind will go down the drain from inaction."

"We need to set an example," Harry suggested. "We need to act as if we believe even if we don't. It's a twist on Pascal's wager with God. If the world can't be saved, whether we do anything or not doesn't matter. But if it can be saved, acting like it can be saved might help make that happen. I'm worried about today's teenagers growing up with doom-and-gloom news and raised by parents who expect disaster. To save mankind, we don't need more facts. We need more fiction, the truth of fiction. We need stories that can help the next generation to believe in love, in life, in the future. Stories are how we give shape to our lives, how we try to make sense of random events."

"So, do you have such a story?" asked Adolph. "The floor is yours, dear sir. And the ceiling, too, if you need it."

"Maybe the situation isn't hopeless," Harry answered. "Maybe what mankind needs is a major threat, something immediate rather than long term, to wake us out of complacency.

"Beth and I watched the *Movie Under the Stars* last night—*The Martian* with Matt Damon. When the movie ended, we went up to the jogging trail and looked at the stars. No clouds. No moon. No city lights or air pollution to obscure the view. I had never seen so many stars. I've always thought that space travel will be like ship travel hundreds of years ago—venturing over vast distances into the unknown. The awareness of how small and insignificant we are in the vastness of time and space. Wondering if life has a purpose and, if so, what it might be or how we might find it.

"We got to talking. And when we got back to our cabin, we wrote our ideas down, hoping to share them with you. I don't know whether this is an essay, a short story, or the first chapter of a novel. Here goes."

Harry: Pop Goes the Universe

Harry began, "'Let me get this straight,' said Ron Wellek professor of astrophysics and cosmology. 'You're talking about a conclusion you've derived from online data. This is like detecting the gravity waves generated when black holes collide. For the sake of argument, I can accept that eventually the universe will come to an end. I can accept that the beginning of that process is about to start. But the odds of such an event starting in the vicinity of our solar system are infinitesimally small. Even if a destructive force field were to be triggered, the odds are great that it wouldn't reach Earth for billions of years. Your theory is interesting, but the danger you describe isn't likely to have any effect on our lives.'

"Roger, a sophomore taking Astronomy 101 explained, 'This isn't a matter of a force field propagating at the speed of light. In that case, in the vastness of the universe, the odds that it would start anywhere near here are negligible, and it could be billions of years before the force struck here. But no. Space-time itself is going to collapse and hence it will take no time at all for everything to end.

"'Professor, you explained in your lectures that the expansion of the universe is like a bubble expanding. As the bubble expands, the surface area gets larger. And while movement along the surface is limited by the speed of light, the expansion of the bubble — the expansion of space-time itself — is not so limited. That's how the universe got so large so fast.

"'Thirteen point seven billion years ago, at the Big Bang, this universe began expanding. There may have been other universes. There may be other universes right now. Nearly all of them burst and end in nanoseconds. By chance, among all the infinite possibilities in all of eternity, this Big Bang led to a set of physical laws that led to a self-sustaining universe capable of expanding and evolving the way ours has.

"You told us all that. And, I believe, astronomers agree on that today.

"'But the more something expands, the thinner the surface gets. Then it pops. My idea is as simple as that. When the bubble pops, the end of everything happens in an instant. By my calculations, that will happen in three years and twenty-seven days.'

"'You mean ...'

"'Yes, pop goes the universe.'

"'Am I to take it that you're waving a sign saying, *the end of the world is nigh*?' the professor laughed.

"'I'm saying *the end of the universe is nigh*. Nothing left. No dystopic world with caveman conditions. There is no afterward. And it wouldn't matter if we had emigrated to Mars. Nothing everywhere. The end of everywhere. The end of where. The end of time and space. Nada.

"'Imagine God is a child blowing bubbles. Most of the bubbles burst right away, but one grows for thirteen point seven billion years, which, to Him, is a short time. The bigger it gets, the thinner its surface gets. And it must expand because there's nothing around it. Something expands to fill nothing. So sooner or later it's so thin that it must burst. And God, like a child, claps his hands with glee to see that. And the universe, our universe, all of it, is gone, instantly.'

"'So what?' asked the Professor. 'If it's all going to be over, it will all be over, whether we know that it's coming or not. By your reasoning there's nothing we can do to stop it.'

"'But we're meant to know that it's going to happen.'

"'Meant to know? What do you mean by that? Meant by whom?'

"'The timing is too perfect. In all of the thirteen point seven billion years since the Big Bang, this will happen at the moment when man has evolved and has developed technology to the point that he can figure out that this is about to happen. That's an incredible coincidence. I don't believe in coincidences. There has to be a reason for this; and if there's a reason for this, then there's a reason for life and consciousness to have existed, a reason for there to be mankind, a reason for there to be you and me. Then everything makes sense.'

"'You make no sense at all, my boy,' the Professor objected. 'Will you celebrate how brilliant you are when everything ends? Congratulations. But you won't be around to celebrate. You and everyone and everything will no longer exist!'

"'You don't get it, professor. This is a quantum thing. Knowing that this is going to happen changes the conditions of the experiment. Knowing matters. Knowing may be all that matters. Maybe us knowing what is about to happen will change the physical conditions of the universe, and it won't happen.'

"'Are you in therapy, boy?'

"'Therapy is the other piece of this. Even if we can't change the physical conditions by knowing, knowing will change us, change what we believe, what we expect, how we behave. Knowing, with certainty, that the world will end on a particular day will change how we act now, how we act every day remaining to us, will transform mankind. And that may be the purpose of the end—redemption, renewal, self-awareness.'

"'And then total oblivion?'

"'Pascal's gamble version 2.0. Do you believe in the imminent end of the universe? If you don't believe, that makes no difference. It will end with or without your belief. But if you do believe, you will change your behavior, everyone will change their behavior, and the world will be transformed.'

"'For better or for worse? What the hell difference will their behavior make if there's no future if everything ends?'

"'Try a thought experiment,' suggested Roger. 'Einstein loved those, like Jesus loved parables. Imagine that you have cancer. There's no chance of a cure. You'll be dead in a year. Would you want to know? And how would knowing affect your behavior in your final days? If you don't know, you'll fritter away your time on things that you don't need to do and that don't mean anything to you. If you do know, you won't want to do things that you consider a waste of time and you won't start things that you won't be able to finish. Maybe you'll do whatever you can for your family and friends, so they'll be better off when you're gone. Maybe you'll try to make the world a better place. And maybe you'll try to ease your mind and achieve inner peace.

"'Now let's turn that thought experiment up a notch. Everyone is going to end at the same time as you. There will be no family, no friends, no world after you. What do you do in the remaining time?

"'I'm not talking about the *Rapture*, some biblical *End of Days*, with God and Satan and the *Saved* and the *Damned*. You can't save your soul by doing good deeds between now and then. There's no quid pro quo, no bargain with God—if I do this, I get that. There's no soul in this scenario. Everything just ends. What do you do with the time you have left? How does that belief change what you value, the meaning of life to you?

"'You could call this the fundamental moral question. If this were the case, what would your values be, what would you do? If there were no future at all and no soul and no God to bargain with, what would you do?

"'In the broader scheme of things, everything may start over again. This universe may be just a stage in a much larger game. Peek-a-boo. Only you won't be around for the next stage. And there will be no memory of you or of anything you have done or of mankind or of the entire universe. The sequel to the Big Bang is the Little Pop.

"'What will you do if you believe, with absolute certainty, that everything will cease to exist on a designated day three years from now? Believing or not believing makes a huge difference. If you believe, should you tell those you know and love? Do you have a moral obligation to tell everyone? What are the consequences if you don't tell them? And what are the consequences if you do?

"'Now I've passed the baton to you, Professor. I've done my duty. The responsibility is yours, not mine. You have to decide to tell or not to tell.'

"'What do you mean?'

"'I'm just a kid. No one would believe me no matter what I might say—not my friends, not my parents, much less the world. But you're a renowned scientist. People will listen to you, and even more people will listen to the people who listen to you. If you tell this tale, whether it's true or not, the world will believe and believing will change the world. That's your responsibility. That weight is on your shoulders now. Thank you, Professor.'"

Day Six: At Sea, Formal Night

If only life were as simple as Harry made it sound. He only had to worry about the classic threats to humanity: nuclear war, over-population, and climate change. He didn't believe that *pop goes the universe* theory. That was his idea of humor. He believed in the future of mankind and in the motivational power of story. He had no notion that mankind was actually on the brink of a different kind of immediate disaster, a global pandemic.

I wish I could believe in the future the way he did. I wish I could believe that once again there will be romance and love, and life will once again be well worth living.

On the other hand, maybe there's a positive spin to what's happening now. Maybe this threat will change how we think and how we act, and, in the long run, we'll be better for it. Maybe it'll put an end to the three previous threats. Maybe from the constraints on romance, population growth will slow. And maybe the pandemic will force us to recognize the interdependence of all nations, lessening the chance of war, much less nuclear war. As for climate change, just a few months of industrial shutdown have improved air quality. The sun now shines in Los Angeles. Maybe we can restart the global economy in stages and in a way that preserves some of what has been gained. But that would require global cooperation, and we have trouble acting as a single nation, much less a single planet.

On Day Six, a sea day on the way back to Fort Lauderdale, when everyone, including Roxanne, had arrived and placed their orders, Randy opened the storytelling with an announcement.

Randy: From Welding to Wedding

"I introduced myself as an artist and museum guard and Jane as a welder turned management consultant,' said Randy. "That wasn't exactly true."

Stan smiled and replied, "That's no surprise. We're here to tell stories. It's not like this is a court of law."

Adolph added, "And that was one hell of a story about how the two of you met, *love at first barf.* Was that fiction?"

"In fact, we met three weeks ago and aren't married, not yet. I advertised on Craig's List for a cabin partner for this cruise. Two can cruise almost as cheaply as one. Single occupancy and double occupancy are the same price. You pay separate gratuities and port fees. That means it's not free for the second person, but it's dirt cheap compared to a week's lodging in a fine hotel, plus all your food and entertainment, plus the attraction of the ports of call. What a deal.

"I was planning to go on this cruise alone. Then I realized I could act as if I were a wealthy man, a *deep-pockets* sugar daddy. I could offer all of this for free to a lady willing to share a cabin with me for a week. I thought I'd be swamped with applicants. Nothing. Nada. My sister looked at the ad and said it sounded creepy. No woman in her right mind would agree to share a cabin with a stranger, much less somebody creepy enough to place such an ad. She thought I came across as a loser, someone who couldn't get a woman any other way.

"Then Jane called. We met at Starbucks. We swapped life stories, like we were on a Match date. She said that she found me attractive and that she liked my imagination. She thought she could trust me. But there was no way she was going to be my rent-for-a-week whore on the bargain plan. She would pay her half of the expenses, and we would sleep in separate beds. The double beds in the cabins are really a pair of twin beds pushed together and sheeted together. We would have the room steward separate them. We could role-play to strangers, pretend we were married, inventing backstories for ourselves. We could wear matching shirts and dance together. But no hanky-panky. If we had a good time together on the cruise, we could date when we got home. It would be that way or no way at all. That was fine with me.

"We had a great time together for the first couple days. You guys were great. We loved hearing your stories and making up stories of our own. She and I were glad to have found one another, but we were just friends. That changed a couple nights ago."

"What happened?" I prompted.

"Dickens had an expression for it: spontaneous combustion. One minute we were lying in separate twin beds, talking about our day. The next minute we were tearing one another's clothes off and couldn't have enough of one another.

"We're getting married tomorrow morning, and we'll honeymoon on this ship. We've signed on for the next week, the Western Caribbean."

"Rinaldo," called Adolph. "Did you hear that? We need champagne tonight and a cake tomorrow. Charge it to my room."

"Will do, sir. With pleasure, sir."

After congratulations and repeated toasts, finishing off two bottles of champagne, we asked for details about the wedding.

"You're all invited, of course," said Randy. "Please join us on the jogging path at ten tomorrow morning. We'll still be in international waters then. The captain will do the honors. We'll take care of the state-side paperwork later. Jane and I will both start at the stern, and we'll run down opposite sides the full length of the ship, and run into one another's arms near the bridge, where the captain will say the words."

I asked, "Are Jane and Randy your real names?"

"Of course not." Randy smiled. "We're Lois and Clark."

"Like the Superman TV series?" I asked.

"Yes, by chance. The names do sound good together. I'm an actuary and Lois is a real estate agent."

"And will Jane, I mean Lois, take your last name, the traditional way?"

"No," he answered with a smile. "I'll take hers, and she'll take mine. I've never heard of doing it that way, but why not?"

"It's a different way of playing the game," added Jane, now Lois. "And that's the name of my story for tonight, *The Name Game*."

Lois: The Name Game

She began, "Once upon a time, in the old country, there was a young woman named Luba who dared to stand up for herself. She wouldn't be her father's property. She wouldn't be a husband's property. She would be an independent woman. She turned down every suitor her parents suggested. She wouldn't so much as talk to the village matchmaker. She would make a living on her own. She didn't need a man.

"When her father decided the family would emigrate to America, she went along. That was fine. It would be easier to be an independent woman in America.

"Her father talked the family next door into going with them. He had wanted her to marry their son Ivan. Luba didn't mind that Ivan would be along for the voyage. He was nice enough. They could talk and play cards on the ocean crossing. Then he'd go his way and she hers.

"When they got to Ellis Island, her father played what he thought was his trump card. He got the registrar to give him the name *Unpronounceable*. Not Liebowitz or Finkelstein or something hard to say. Literally, the surname he chose was *Unpronounceable*.

"Luba was furious. 'My name is to be *Luba Unpronounceable*? Are you kidding me? That's no name. That's an abomination. Go back and set it right.'

"'What's done is done,' her father insisted. 'American bureaucracy. That's the way it will have to be for your mother and me. But you, my dear one, you have a choice. You could marry this fine young man who you've known all your life, and then you would be *Mrs. Cantor*, instead of *Miss Unpronounceable*.'

"Much to her father's surprise and delight, she agreed. She wanted to marry Ivan but had held back because she didn't want to lose face. Her father's trick with the name gave her the excuse she needed. She could marry the man she wanted, get a name she liked, and still she would be an independent woman."

I chuckled and asked Jane, "So what's your new last name going to be?"

"Lane."

"You're kidding us again, right? *Lois Lane*? And is Randy going to be *Clark Kent*?"

"Exactly," she affirmed, taking Randy's hand. "That's the gospel truth, so help me gods of Krypton."

"And you're really getting married?" I asked for confirmation. "That's not a joke? You want us on the jogging trail at ten in the morning?"

"Amen, brother."

"Delightful," Adolph grinned. "All this talk of made-up stories reminds me of one told by an old friend of mine, a story that might or might not be true."

Adolph: Swampland

"When Morris' uncle died," said Adolph, "he drove up to North Carolina to clear out the house. In a box full of papers, he found old deeds to land in Florida. Back in the 1920s, his uncle had fallen for a get-rich-quick scam and bought land that turned out to be worthless swamp. Morris figured that maybe he could find people who were just as gullible now as his uncle was back then. Maybe he could fool someone else and turn those old deeds into cash.

"He came up with a story, sheer fantasy, that Disney was thinking of building a Disneyland on the East Coast and was going to buy land around Orlando. Morris whispered that story to some friends of his in New York, who whispered it to friends of theirs, thinking this was an inside scoop, a sure thing, but hush-hush. In a couple days, Morris had an offer for that swamp land for a good price. That's when he realized that this fairytale he had made up had potential. Instead of selling the land he had deeds for, he decided to buy all the land in that area that he could.

"It would have been impossible to find the owners because they were scattered across the country. They had been swindled into buying the land like Morris' uncle was back in the twenties. They figured it was worthless, and they had probably torn up or misplaced the deeds. But, as Morris soon learned, he didn't need to find those owners. None of them had paid the taxes, so the town had confiscated the property. That land was sitting idle, useless, unwanted. Morris bought it all from the town for practically nothing.

"Then Morris set about to spread that same Disney rumor on a larger scale. The tabloids picked up the story, and he got lots of calls from would-be buyers. He put them off, waiting for the price to go up in a bidding war.

"Then he got a call from Walt Disney himself. Walt flew Morris to Hollywood, for a face-to-face talk. Walt had heard the rumor. He knew that Morris had started it. He was tempted to turn Morris over to the police for fraud. Legally, Morris was probably clear. He hadn't run ads. He hadn't put anything in writing claiming that Walt wanted that land.

He had just spread the rumor. But Walt could cost him a fortune in legal fees. And Walt could put a stop to the rumor by a public announcement denying it, which would have left Morris with lots of worthless swampland.

"Instead, Walt offered him a deal. Walt liked the idea of an East Coast Disneyland. And Orlando looked like a great location. He couldn't expand in Anaheim. If he could get a big enough tract of land in Orlando, he could build a resort destination, not just an amusement park. He could get revenue for hotels, restaurants, and shopping. So, he gave Morris a choice. Either Morris could sell him all that land, at a fair price, comparable to what an orange grove would sell for, or Walt would announce that he had no such plans, and Morris would get nothing."

"Why didn't we hear about this?" I asked.

"That was part of the deal—a non-disclosure agreement. Walt wanted to get full credit for this brilliant business idea."

"And how do we know that you're not lying?" asked Roxanne.

Randy started laughing. "I'll bet that Adolph has outdone us all at lying."

Adolph smiled and winked.

"But maybe I can do you one better," boasted Randy, now Clark. "I call this story *Shades of Gay*." He picked up his glass of merlot and drank it all in a series of swallows without putting the glass down. Then he launched into an apology.

Lois and Clark: Shades of Gay

"Jane, I mean Lois, and I aren't very sociable," he explained. "We don't start up conversations with strangers, nor do they approach us. You folks here at this table are the only people we've spoken to since we got on the ship. That means we haven't heard any stories other than the ones you've told us. We know nothing of the loves and lives of the thousands of strangers around us. But we do enjoy talking to one another, speculating about who these people might be and what they might have done. And we've fabricated some gossipy tales based on the slenderest of clues."

"Well, bring it on, Randy or Clark," Adolph encouraged him. "Share your baseless gossip. What you say here is just for us and anyone we might tell, and anyone they might tell until the end of time. Have no qualms. Slander to your heart's content. Those strangers will always be strangers to you and to us."

Clark pointed to his wine glass, and Rinaldo went to fetch the wine steward to deliver a refill. Then he began, "After dinner last night, Lois and I went dancing in the Piazza. There we saw a couple that puzzled us. It's common to see gay couples on the dance floor. But, in this case, we couldn't agree on which one was the man and which the woman, or if they were both women or both men. But they danced beautifully together, each anticipating the other's moves. Based on nothing more than our observations, we came up with a few scenarios."

Lois picked up the story from there, "Imagine a man falls in love with a woman and the woman in love with him, but she's gay and he can't turn her on. He becomes a cross-dresser out of love for her, to please her. He feels unnatural in that role, but he loves her dearly and would do anything for her."

Clark continued, "In our second variation, the man isn't just cross-dressing. He's acted the part of a woman so well that she believes he is a woman. For the months that they've been going together, he has pleasured her with hands and mouth and devices, contriving role-play situations in which she never sees him naked. When she drinks too much at her sister's wedding and passes out in their hotel room, he gets

139

carried away and makes love to her naturally while she's unconscious. Having never anticipated this situation, he doesn't have a condom. Later, when she has morning sickness, he suspects that she's pregnant. She hasn't a clue, thinking she has never made love to a man. Now, on this cruise, he's trying to build up the courage to tell her, hoping that she'll forgive him for impregnating her."

"And, also, for being a man," Lois added.

"In the third variation," said Clark, "like the second, she doesn't know that he's a man. She told him that she wished they could have a baby together. He tells her that thanks to the marvels of modern medicine an egg from a woman can be impregnated with genetic material from another woman, and the embryo can be implanted in either of them, for her to carry the fetus to term and have a natural birth that would be the genetic child of both of them. She agrees to try that. Unbeknownst to her, he colludes with a doctor friend. When she's anesthetized in the doctor's office, he makes love with her naturally. In this version, she's pregnant now, and knows that she's pregnant and that her partner is a biological parent of her child. But she has no idea he's a man and no idea that he tricked her this way. He hopes that when he confesses, she'll realize that he did this out of love for her."

Lois continued, "This morning, in the elevator, going up to the Lido deck, we chanced upon that same couple. Earlier, when we had seen them dancing together, they were dressed androgynously. You couldn't guess their gender from their clothes. This time they were dressed traditionally as a man and a woman. Our curiosity overcame our unsociability. We joined them for breakfast in the buffet. We learned that the woman isn't gay, and she knew all along that he was a man. She thought that he was sexually confused, but she loved him so much that she pretended to be gay, finding that sexual ambiguity turned him on. We guessed right about the pregnancy. She's delighted that they're having a baby together and that now that they have been honest with one another, they can have a normal life together."

"Bravo," Adolph cheered. "So, you did meet them, and you figured out the mystery."

Lois and Clark laughed. "Of course not. We made the whole thing up."

Beth added, "Sometimes what happens to change the course of lives is beyond truth or fiction and is more than coincidence."

"And do you have such a story, Miss Beth?" asked Adolph.

"Of course," she agreed with a smile. "Harry's mention of Lainie, our friend from Perth, Australia, with her brightly colored hair, made me remember our friends Pete and Lucy.

Beth: I Dream of Lucy

"Pete was a software engineer, working for DEC, the minicomputer company, which was once the second largest computer company in the world with 140,000 employees. It's now defunct. At DEC, he had access to the Internet, in the days before the Web and public access. Back then, the Internet was little more than email and file transfer among government agencies, research universities, and computer companies. Of course, the conversations that took place over that first global network were not limited to business. News groups grew which connected people with common interests, and those interests spanned the full range of human activity, including the paranormal.

"Many people were fascinated by the concept of *dream space*, a variation of a traditional belief of Australian aborigines, that when we sleep, we all go to the same separate realm of being, where dreams can be shared. People can meet there, and what happens there can impact ordinary life.

"Thousands of people with Internet access agreed to participate in a global experiment to try to prove the existence of *dream space*. Everyone was supposed to, before going to sleep, imagine a phone booth in the desert near Alice Springs, in the Australian Outback. Beforehand, they were all supposed to shift their sleep habits so they could all go to sleep at about the same time, wherever they lived. Since the bulk of the participants lived in the Eastern Time Zone of the U. S., the base time there would be between midnight and 3 a.m.. That worked out to between 1:30 and 4:30 p.m. later that same day at Alice Springs. In their dreams, they were all supposed to go to that imaginary phone booth, to leave messages there and to look for and memorize messages they found there. The following morning, anyone who saw and remembered a message, was supposed to contact the person who wrote it and then notify the entire news group.

"Pete was psyched. He had read Bruce Chatwin's book *Songlines* about the aborigines, their way of life, and their beliefs. For the month before the experiment, he practiced focusing on a single object as he was falling asleep in hopes that that object would become embedded in his dreams. Also, night after night he set his alarm clock for 3 a.m. He was pleased that the alarm often woke him in the middle of a dream, and he built the habit of immediately writing down every detail he could remember of that dream. This was in the days before the Web, so he couldn't just go online to see images of phone booths. Instead, he bought a printed book of photographs of phone booths. On the night of the experiment, for hours before midnight, he stared at every page of that book, over and over again.

"He fell into a dream that began with him in a phone booth in New York City. As a sixth grader on a school outing, he had gotten separated from the group. He had been staring at a cute girl when he should have been climbing onto a bus. This was before there were cellphones, and he had been well trained not to talk to strangers. He had walked for blocks until he finally found a phone booth with a working phone, so he could call for help. And he stayed there in the booth, afraid to go out on the street again, until his dad came to pick him up. To keep from panicking, while he waited, he had read repeatedly all the graffiti and names and phone numbers on the walls of the booth. His dream during the experiment began with him in that same phone booth and reading that same graffiti, while busy people rushed by on the sidewalk outside.

"Then the dream cut to a phone booth in a desert. It was a different phone booth. The graffiti and names and numbers were gone. The telephone receiver was missing, and the metal-clad wire that had once connected a receiver to the phone box hung loosely. The phone could never have worked because there were no wires extending out of the booth and there were no telephone poles anywhere in sight. There was nothing but flat desert as far as the eye could see. He felt like he was in a Stephen King movie.

"Then he realized that there were dozens of pieces of paper stuck to the outside of the booth. He stepped out to look at them. The paper was wet. It must have rained. It may have been one of the legendary mid-desert downpours in which people sometimes drown. The ink on the pieces of paper had run. The writing was illegible. He checked carefully, tearing them off, one by one, frustrated to have come so far, to be so close to the goal, and yet to fail.

"Then he realized that some notes had been stuck on top of other notes. Under three wet illegible messages he found one that was dry and clear. There was a complete phone number with the 617 area code which meant Boston, where he lived. The note it was signed *Lucy*.

"His alarm clock went off. He woke up with that number in his head.

"He tripped getting out of bed and crawled to his desk where he wrote down that number and the name *Lucy*.

"His mind was racing. This was revolutionary. This could be tangible proof of the existence of *dream space*. That would mean not only that people could share dream experiences, but also that the soul is separate from the body, and as ancient Greeks had believed, that it leaves the body when you sleep and returns to it when you wake. And if there is a soul that's separate from the body, then maybe it can persist after the body dies, in *dream space* or in some other realm of being, and perhaps it can move to another body. One mind-bending possibility after another raced through his mind. but all of this depended on the information being accurate. There had to be someone named *Lucy* at that number, someone who had participated in the experiment.

"Pete tried to calm down. He got dressed. He had breakfast. He lifted the receiver of his telephone but hesitated to dial the number. Discovery and proof that all of mankind shared a common *dream space* would be a monumental discovery. That realm might transcend ordinary space, like a portal enabling him to instantaneously travel vast distances. And it might even transcend time, making time travel possible. He was elated by the possibilities. He felt privy to the secrets of the universe. And he didn't want to dash it by dialing that number and hearing a mechanical recording saying that the number was out of service or there was no such number.

"He went for a run to calm down, but turned around before he had gone a block, and raced back and dialed. It rang. No answer, but also no recording saying that it was a bad number.

"After five rings, it went to an answering machine. The recording said, 'Hello. This is Lucy. Please leave a message after the beep.'

"Lucy! Her name was Lucy!

"He left a message. 'Hello, Lucy. I got your number and your name from a phone booth in Australia. I wasn't there physically. I was there in *dream space*. Australian aborigines believe we all go to an alternate reality when we sleep. We all go to the same alternate reality. Thousands of people from around the world planned an experiment communicating over a global computer network. We performed that experiment last night, trying to dream of a phone booth in the Australian Outback, near Alice Springs. In our dreams we were to leave messages at the phone booth in the hope that someone else from our group would see that message and remember it when waking and make contact with the sender, confirming that *dream space* is real. You are the proof that it's real. We have to talk. We have to meet.'

"Lucy called back an hour later. She lived a couple miles away from him, in Dedham, Massachusetts. They met for lunch at a sandwich shop in downtown Dedham. She was intrigued. She had never heard of the experiment. She had nothing to do with that message appearing in his dream. But her phone number was unlisted. And he didn't know anyone she knew. And yet he had her name and number.

"They were still talking at 8 p.m. when the shop closed. They had forgotten to eat supper. They weren't hungry. They weren't thirsty. They still wanted to talk. They went to her place. They fell in love. They married. They had three boys and a cocker spaniel.

"And never again did either of them return to the phone booth in *dream space*."

Thelma: Shipboard Retirement

Thelma spoke next. "Stan and I have something to announce. We've decided on a shipboard retirement. We met another couple who are doing that, so we looked into the details. We're getting on in years, and the hassles of everyday life are getting to be more than we like. We were thinking about assisted living, but that costs at least ten and maybe as much as fifteen thousand dollars a month. Cruising is a hell of a lot cheaper and a hell of a lot more fun. We'll keep a one-bedroom condo in Miami as our address and place of residence. We'll stop there every couple months. We'll sell our house in Jersey and get rid of the useless stuff we've accumulated. We'll sell our cars and cancel the car insurance. Then we'll go on one cruise after another. We'll shop for discounted deals on vacationstogo.com. If you're flexible and can make last-minute plans, you can cruise for fifty to a hundred dollars a day. Where can you find a luxury resort hotel, including great food and entertainment, for less than a hundred dollars a day? Cruising isn't just for honeymoons. It can be a way of life."

Abe: Self-Storage

"My head is spinning now," I said. "These stories, these identities turning this way and that. These different flavors of reality. I need to get my bearings.

"Randy—I still think of you as Randy—I was used to you being an artist and a museum guard. I can't imagine you as an actuary. Yes, people change, but not that fast. When you introduced yourself, I was reminded of Reggie, an old friend of mine who also was an artist and a museum guard. He died a few years ago.

"Actually, Reggie died twice. The first time, he was nineteen. He had meningitis. The pain was excruciating. His death was a welcome respite from pain. As he remembered it, he rose from his body and hovered above. He looked down on himself in the hospital bed and on the doctor and nurse who were scrambling to revive him.

"Even then he had the visual instincts of an artist, and he was intrigued to see himself from that perspective, to see all of life from a distance, from above, detached, seeing the loss of life, even the loss of his own life, with curiosity rather than fear.

"When the doctors revived him, they told him that his heart had stopped for over three minutes. Technically he had died.

"To him, that experience felt like it lasted for hours, and that vision of himself from above became the defining experience of his life. Over the following decades, he returned to it repeatedly in his paintings.

"His work is labelled *surrealistic*, but it's unique.

"Many of his paintings show crowds of heads, the heads huge in proportion to the bodies or the bodies not visible at all. The heads are oblong rectangles, rounded at the corners. He drew sharp black outlines around areas of flat color, with eyes and noses and mouths drawn over. Sometimes he stacked heads on top of heads, like floors of an apartment building, or crowded heads together, with no room left on the canvas to show their bodies. In one painting, some heads are right-side up, others sideways, others upside down, in a social situation that calls to mind Eliot's *Love Song of Alfred Prufrock*, where women come and go, talking of Michelangelo.

"The figures in his oil paintings are often cartoon-like, and some of his works are pen and ink cartoon drawings. Much of his work is ironic, mocking, and at the same time sad. His clowns are sad clowns, their painted-on smiles emphasizing their underlying despair.

"The most human and touching of his works is a painting entitled *Piaf,* which is actually a portrait of his wife, Elle.

"His most cheerful and hopeful paintings are of white dancing figures, souls set free from their bodies, floating against a black sky with a white moon and white stars.

"In his *X-Ray Eyes* a disembodied black head with glasses sits on a table, as if it were a crystal ball, and stares at a woman sitting in a chair, facing him, and staring back at him, with a red coat opened wide, revealing her skeleton as in an X-ray.

"He called his doll-like figures *puppets* or *marionettes.* Fate was the puppet master. At his funeral, the rabbi said that the puppets were held by *divine strings,* but with some degree of free will.

"That image of him looking down at himself after he died for the first time makes me think of advertisements for *self-storage.* When we are young, I think we all store images of ourselves. We have an idea of who we should be, and we compare that to the self we are and the self we're likely to become. That helps us get back on track when we stray, helps us avoid losing ourselves in the everyday hassles of the world. Like Wordsworth, who said that the child is father to the man, and that the world is too much with us late and soon.

"When we fall in love and marry, we can take on that role for one another. Babs became the keeper of my sense of self. She was my compass. When she died, I lost not just her, I lost that image of myself as well."

Adolph: Mae Again

Adolph sighed. "If only every love story had a happy ending. I told you about Mae, my Mae. I told you that she died. Gather ye rosebuds while ye Mae. I don't talk about it, because I was a coward at the end. The thought of death terrified me.

"Mae had cancer, and for a year I was with her every step of the way. I saw her after her surgery as soon as she came out of recovery. I held her hand for hours as she got chemo. I cooked for her. I bathed her. I was with her every minute. Then I cracked. I couldn't take it anymore— not the labor of it, but rather the reminder of death, day after day being in the physical presence of death and being reminded of my own mortality. I couldn't take it.

"I hired a caregiver to fill in for me, and I took off. I went to the racetrack five days running and stayed in a cheap motel nearby. I didn't tell anyone where I'd gone.

"I lost everything. I drained our bank account with our credit cards. I was thinking magically. If fate had screwed us over, killing Mae like this, there had to be some counterbalancing luck. We were due for a longshot win like the win that got us together in the first place. I was going to keep betting until I got a winner, a big winner. And I did. With my last two dollars, I bought a trifecta ticket and won a hundred thousand dollars.

"I rushed home to tell Mae and found out that she had died while I was gone. In fact, she had died the day I left. By the time I got home, she had already been buried. Nobody had known how to reach me. I have nothing more to say. That's enough. That's more than enough."

"Hearing that, I can't help but think of Ralph," said Roxanne.

"Ralph?" asked Adolph.

"My husband, my only husband. He died thirty years ago."

Roxanne: Love Without Borders

"Ralph was a doctor, a cosmetic surgeon," Roxanne explained. "We lived near New Haven, Connecticut. He did nose jobs and facelifts, which brought in the money, but he also did reconstructive surgery. He took great pride in the work he did for children with cleft lip and cleft palate." She turned to me. "Abe, Adolph told me that your son had that condition and went through those surgeries.

"Well, Ralph and I were happy. We were well-off. We were in our early thirties with long, happy lives ahead of us.

"Then one day, without consulting me, Ralph signed up for *Operation Smile*. That's like *Doctors Without Borders*, only specializing in children with cleft. Doctors volunteer to go to third world countries to perform facial surgery for free, transforming the lives of children who otherwise would be disfigured and outcast for life. That's a noble cause. But this was my husband, and this was my life as well as his that he was gambling on the spur of the moment.

"They sent him to India. I wouldn't go along. I was afraid. If I were to get sick, I wouldn't want to wind up in one of their hospitals. The poor health care, the very reason he was going there, was the reason I couldn't go with him.

"He told me he needed to do this. He felt guilty making a fortune giving rich ladies face lifts when his skills could make a real difference, rebuilding the faces of children who otherwise would never be able to get the care they needed. Over my protests, over my begging, over my offering to do anything sexual or otherwise that could change his mind, he went.

"He worked in the slums of Calcutta. Kolkata they call it now. I can't get used to the name changes. Population over four million. Think of the movie *Slumdog Millionaire*. Think of Mother Teresa. I guess he wanted to be Father Teresa. I just wanted him to be my husband Ralph.

"He did his do-gooder thing. He signed on for six months, and he was dead before two months had passed. He caught some horrible disease that's endemic to that part of the world and that we don't have here. He died of it despite having been vaccinated against it.

"I couldn't forgive him for that, for the selfishness of what he had done, killing himself like that and leaving me behind, not thinking of me at all, just thinking of those children. I was mad at him for not loving me enough to stay with me, to be safe with me, so we could get old together and die together, naturally, when our time came. And I was mad at myself for being mad at him, for my selfishness.

"I wasn't there with him when he fell sick. and I wasn't there with him when he weakened and died. I couldn't comfort him. I couldn't tell him I loved him. I never even saw his dead body. Because the illness that killed him was contagious, they cremated him immediately. And I was so mad at him I said I didn't want his ashes even if they were disinfected. In anger, I said, 'Dump the ashes in the Ganges,' and they did, literally, before I had time to change my mind.

"I was thirty and he thirty-five when he died, thirty years ago. I never wanted to get close to another man. I couldn't stand the pain of loss again.

"We had one daughter, Janine.

"Here on this ship, seeing old men, in wheelchairs, maybe near death, I wondered what it might be like to be with one of them, to care for him, to care about him, to make him happy in his final days, perhaps as a penance, perhaps because I hadn't been there for Ralph, because I hadn't dared share the danger with him in India.

"Yes, seeing men in wheelchairs, I thought of my own dad, too, near the end, when he was in a wheelchair. But the idea passed through my mind that I could connect with one of those lonely old men and make him less lonely, adopt him like adopting a rescue dog. Maybe I was being selfish, wanting to care about someone and be with him in his final days, and wanting someone to care about me and be with me at the end, given that my end may well be near.

"Of course, an outsider, someone who didn't know me, seeing me get friendly with an old man like that would think I was some kind of predator, a vulture trying to seduce an old man, soon to die, for his money, deliberately looking for a man with *deep pockets*. And it hit a raw nerve in me when another woman, my own age, came after me accusing me of that, defending her territory because she had already staked out, as her target, the old man I was being nice to.

"Love and death, death and love. Death is too much with us late and soon."

I followed up. "Many of the stories that all of you have told here have rung true to me as if I had heard them before or had experienced something like them in another life. I have ITP, like Harry. And my father had a stroke without a blood clot, like Harry's father. A cousin of mine had an experience like the one that Harry described, basing his life on a misunderstanding. And Babs and I participated in that *dream space* experiment, but neither of us found the phone booth.

"I feel a bond with all of you and with the stories you've told, as if you were all in some sense a part of me. It's as if I could have lived your lives and the lives of the characters in your stories, as if we all have the potential to become different people and to live different lives, that different circumstances lead to this or that potential coming out in us. In some sense, each of us is all of us, hence we can empathize and get involved in one another's stories. We're all connected in ways that defy science, and when we find the one we love and who loves us, the two of us become one, and that bond is not just until death do us part—there is no parting.

"This must sound looney. but since Babs died, for me the boundary between what's real and what's imagined has blurred. What all the evidence around me confirms—that she is dead, gone, never to return—can't be true, so how can everything else I perceive be true? Of course, I'm in denial. I'll probably always be in denial over this."

Abe: Ghost Stories

"Babs and I used to see ghosts in our bedroom," I continued. "I'd see them two or three times a month, Babs two or three times a week. She woke me up and pointed and I'd look hard, but I could never see hers, and she could never see mine. Afterwards, we'd talk about what we had seen. These weren't dreams, at least not ordinary dreams. They took place on a different plane of being.

"Babs saw people she had never seen before standing and looking at her or approaching her. The visions never spoke. They always exited through the shut sliding doors to our clothes closet and the under-eaves storage. Only rarely did the ghosts act threatening.

"We joked about the house being haunted. Then we took a short tourist trip to London. Remember the story that Beth told about *The Duke and Duchess of Coney Island*? Beth mentioned Hyde Park and the corner that used to be called Tyburn, the site of public hangings in the distant past. Babs and I stayed at that same hotel on Bayswater that Beth described in her story. And the first night in the hotel room, Babs woke up screaming that there were three men, dressed in old-style workman clothes, sitting huddled and frightened on the floor in the corner. The next morning, we found out that the pub next door had been the last stop for prisoners on their way to be hung at Tyburn. Apparently, our visions of ghosts weren't just a matter of us living in a haunted house. She could see them elsewhere. She was particularly sensitive.

"My experiences in our bedroom would have been far more unsettling and frightening to me if Babs hadn't had hers. I'd see the room exactly as it was in the dark, the shapes of solid walls and furniture clear from moonlight or streetlights through the windows. Miniature human-like apparitions would float in midair. Sometimes they'd come alone, sometimes in pairs. They never spoke, and they never seemed sad or malevolent.

"When we first saw them, soon after we moved in, Babs or I would scream, the visions would vanish, and we'd hug to comfort one another. But, over time, we got used to them and took them for granted. We tried unsuccessfully to confirm one another's sightings, but we didn't doubt

157

their reality. We didn't get the sense that these beings meant us harm or that they wished us well. They were aware of us, looking us straight in the eye. But they were in their world, and we were in ours. It was peaceful co-existence, as politicians used to say in the days of the Cold War.

"I had had one sighting like that long before I met Babs, when I was about eight. That time the figures I saw were my parents, tiny, maybe a few inches tall, ballroom dancing together in the air above my bed, near the ceiling, dancing round and round, maybe a waltz, but with no music except in their minds. That time I was terrified. I was wide awake. I could clearly see the room around me. But I couldn't move or speak or scream, though I very much wanted to scream. That went on for what felt like hours. It ended at dawn when the figures disappeared and I could move, but I didn't wake up because I was already awake. I'd been awake the whole time. I never told anyone about that experience until Babs. I told her and she told me of sightings she had had. We had that in common, a belief that there were such beings and that we could sometimes see them.

"Twice, when we were married and had kids, I had a different kind of vision. The window on the north side of our bedroom played a role in both. One time, a man-sized figure rose on the window, not inside or outside, rather like a movie projected on the surface of the glass. First the top of his head appeared, then he continued rising at a slow but steady pace until his upper body filled the window. Then he vanished. By the time I thought to wake Babs, he was gone. That's when I realized that the image I had seen matched a painting my parents had hung in my bedroom when I was a kid. The painting, a reproduction, showed a teenage boy at the steering wheel of a ship, and behind him, guiding him, unbeknownst to him, hovered Jesus. The figure I had seen matched the Jesus in that picture. That time I was scared, very scared. It took a long while for Babs to calm me.

"Another time, through that same window, three thugs, dressed like eighteenth century workmen, like the men Babs had seen in the hotel in London, climbed into the bedroom and came at me, machetes in hand. I screamed and they disappeared. I tried to make sense of that experience as a wakeup call, my unconscious reminding me that I'm mortal and that if there's anything I really want to do, I'd better do it soon.

"Several times since Babs died, sleeping alone, I've woken up screaming, my heart beating dangerously fast, like when the thugs climbed into my room. On those occasions, I didn't remember what scared me. But I felt Babs' presence hovering above me, calming and comforting me. And once or twice I could swear I saw myself through her eyes, looking down at me, like Reggie described seeing himself from above."

Day Seven: Returning to Fort Lauderdale

Today, I had a virtual session with my doctor. I have an infection around my toenail. Before the pandemic, I would have made an appointment, then driven to the doctor's office, where I would have waited in the company of other patients, some with infectious diseases. Instead, this time I connected by way of a cellphone app. The session took two minutes, and the pharmacy will deliver the antibiotic tomorrow.

The technology for that kind of doctor's visit has been around for about fifteen years. The pandemic helped break through the bureaucratic barriers. That's one of the things that isn't likely to go away if and when the pandemic cools down.

We have all quickly abandoned long-established habits and expectations. We are far more flexible and malleable than I would have imagined we could be. Change happens. This pandemic is greatly accelerating the pace of change.

This is a crazy ride we're on, and it's hard to guess what it will lead to. Some of the changes may turn out to be positive. Maybe this is a wakeup call for mankind.

"Rinaldo," Adolph called as dinner started on the seventh and last day. "Champagne for all but me. I'll stick to my cranberry juice. Old habits die hard. And I'm both old and a die hard."

"Cranberry juice for me as well," Beth added.

"And bring the cake now, please," Adolph continued. "As Thelma told us, 'Life's short. Eat dessert first.' The wisdom of the ages. And wisdom ages fast, so bring it quickly please."

Once the glasses were filled, Adolph toasted, "To Lois and Clark. May they go where no man or woman has gone before, finding new sources of mutual joy. And may their love inspire millions of others to marry and to multiply and be fruitful, that mankind not go extinct, but rather carry forth the gospel of love to the planets and the galaxies, forever and ever. Amen."

Beth interrupted, "We're making a start on that. Harry and I are being fruitful."

"Strawberries or grapes?" asked Adolph.

"We're not sure which flavor yet."

"Well, tell us all. Including the news that's not fit to print."

Harry: The Wrong Wedding Gift

"Before we married," Harry explained, "Beth was uptight about the risk of pregnancy, extremely so. She insisted that I use a condom, even though she was on the pill, and had an IUD, and used spermicidal cream as well. If her period was one day late, she'd give herself a pregnancy test, then a second test, then a third. She never had a kind word to say about any of the children we came across. She obsessed about the dangers of over-population. Although she never came out and said so, I had no doubt that she didn't want to have children of her own.

"When I mentioned her anxiety about pregnancy to a friend of mine, who was going to be my best man and who happened to be a urologist, he offered to do a vasectomy for free, as a wedding gift. I myself wanted kids, but since she didn't want them, I was willing to do this for her, because I loved her. It was a sacrifice for me, but well worth it if it was as important to her, as I believed it was.

"I went ahead with the vasectomy, figuring this was a surprise that would delight her when I told her on our wedding night.

"She was furious.

"Now that she was married, she wanted children, lots of them, starting as soon as possible.

"How could I have misunderstood her so badly?

"I went back to my friend, and he did a reverse vasectomy, also a gift.

"But reverse vasectomies don't always work; and even when they do, it can take months before normal function is restored.

"Now she obsessively wanted to become pregnant. I went back repeatedly for tests to find out if the reversal had worked.

"It didn't.

"That was two years ago. The prognosis was that I would never father children."

Beth continued the story.

Beth: New Life

"With the cancer diagnosis," she said, "it was a good thing I wasn't pregnant. The chemo and the radiation that saved me wouldn't have been possible. Sometimes bad things have good outcomes. Unexpected consequences.

"With the cancer behind us, we looked into other options for having children like in vitro and adoption. In vitro was expensive, and our insurance wouldn't pay for it. Adoption, too, was expensive and involved lots of paperwork and a long waiting list. If we wanted a healthy infant, not an older child with serious problems, a rescue kid, we would have to wait for years. We decided to take this trip and postpone deciding.

"I missed a period, but with the treatments I had had, that was no surprise. I didn't think anything of it.

"Then this morning, on a whim, I took a home pregnancy test and hit the jackpot. I'm pregnant."

"Ah," exclaimed Adolph. "New life. Delightful. No wonder you passed on the champagne and chose cranberry juice, like me. I should have guessed. Bravo. Let's drink to Beth and Harry and to Lois and Clark, and to Jane and Randy as well."

"I'll go next," Randy AKA Clark volunteered.

Randy: My Bonnie Lies Over the Ocean

He began his story, "Bonnie and Lew were childhood best friends. When they were ten, he bought a gold-colored plastic ring for a quarter and got down on one knee and asked her if she would marry him some day. She, without hesitation, said yes. A few years later Bonnie's family moved to Australia.

"At first, they corresponded by snail mail. This was before the Web and public email. They wrote each other every day, but it took a week for the letters to arrive. The dialogue was painful for both of them, not so much keeping them in touch as reminding them of their distance, of the fact that they were growing apart, that it was hopeless to try to keep their romance alive from opposite sides of the world. They agreed to stop writing.

"Lew went to college, then he got a job working as a middle manager for a retail chain. He met and dated dozens of girls, none of them seriously, except for Diane, who he thought he wanted to marry,

"The breakup with Diane took him by surprise. He had bought an engagement ring and carefully planned an evening out when he would propose. As he reached into his pocket for the ring box and prepared to kneel, the lights flickered; he blinked; and when he looked at her again, her image blurred, and he couldn't bring her into focus. She was a stranger. Her voice sounded far away and flat. He couldn't decipher what she was saying, and he realized he didn't care what she was saying. He blurted out, 'Will you be my friend?' instead of 'Will you marry me?' He never took the ring out of his pocket; and she, her expectations thwarted, broke up with him on the spot.

"Back at his apartment, he googled Bonnie. He found her address in Sydney and learned that she was unmarried. They exchanged a few emails, but he wasn't good with words. He wanted to see her in person and see if sparks might fly. He would surprise her. He would go by cruise ship, out of San Pedro, the cruise port for Los Angeles. He was afraid of flying. He had that in common with her. He remembered her fears when she had to fly to Australia so long ago.

"Over-anxious, he got to the cruise terminal early while they were disembarking passengers from the previous trip. A woman leaving the terminal looked familiar. He couldn't place her face, but he was intrigued. It would be two hours before he could board. On a whim, he followed her to the long line of people waiting for cabs. It wasn't just her looks, but also her gestures, her gait, her style.

"As he walked past her, he found himself whistling, *My Bonnie lies over the ocean.*

"She looked up, smiled, waved, and said, 'Hi, Lew.'

"He stopped and stared. This was Bonnie, his Bonnie. He was delighted to have miraculously found her. But she was waving with her left hand, and there was a gold ring on her ring finger.

"She stepped forward and added, 'How did you know I was coming? I wanted it to be a surprise.'

"He kept staring at her ring finger.

"She saw where he was looking and held her hand up to his face. 'Yes, stranger. I'm engaged. I've been engaged for fifteen years.'

"She was beaming with joy. The ring was plastic.

"This cruise is their honeymoon."

Adolph broke in, "That's our cue, gentlemen and ladies. Let's raise our glasses once again, to the newlyweds, to the newly knocked up, to the soon-to-be perpetual cruisers, to the man who sees ghosts, and to my fair lady, the fairest of the fair.

"Rinaldo, more champagne and more cranberry juice, if you please. And a story, Rinaldo. You have heard us all. You are one of the initiates of our cult of story. Weave your thoughts and words with ours."

Rinaldo started talking while walking around the table pouring the drinks. "I must admit that hearing you night after night I have thought what I might say, were I a guest at this table. If I may, I'd like to tell a tale about Hawaii."

"Hawaii? Your badge says you're from the Philippines."

"Yes. That is partly true. My father is from Manila, and that is where I was born. But my mother is from the island of Maui, in Hawaii, and her mother was from Australia and her father from Los Angeles. How can you fit so much truth on such a small name tag? And are we not all more than just a name and an address? There's a pair of Hawaiian singers on this cruise. Perhaps you have heard them?"

"Yes," a few of us mumbled between bites of our steak.

"They will be forced to retire after this cruise, as their contract has run out and they, as all lowly crew staff, must retire, without pension, at thirty-five. They will have to start a new life.

"They met on a cruise ship in the Pacific. She was a solo performer of traditional Japanese music and dance, and he was a solo Chinese performer. They fell in love and merged their acts as a Hawaiian duet, and they were fortunate to get one cruise contract after another until now, when they must retire.

"I hear they plan to move to New Jersey, where they were both born. There they will work on his parents' blueberry farm, and sometimes they may perform in Atlantic City. So, while we don't know if there is life after death, it is indeed true that there is life after cruising."

"Is that your story?" asked Adolph. "Just that?"

"Well, I have another story as well, if I may be permitted."

"Yes. Please."

Rinaldo: Maui The God

"The island of Maui in Hawaii was named for a god of that same name. Before Europeans arrived in that part of the world, that god and his legend were also known in New Zealand, nearly five thousand miles from Hawaii, and in Tonga and Tahiti and Samoa — thousands of miles in other directions. In the old days, the only way to travel long distances in the Pacific was by out-rigger canoe. For the legends of Maui to have spread so far, people must have traveled those vast distances in canoes through the open ocean, with no land in sight, where on a clear day, waves can be ten feet high, and on a stormy day the waves can be horrendous. They had no navigational instruments. So how could they have known where they were and where they were going? And in the open ocean, because of the curvature of the Earth, they could only see a few miles to the horizon.

"Imagine the faith and courage it would take to sail and row such a tiny boat in the open ocean with no land in sight and no assurance that they would ever reach land. I'm reminded of what Harry said yesterday about space travel, our place in the universe, and whether life might have a purpose, and what that purpose might be.

"I can't help but wonder. Maybe instead of thousands of people with primitive technology making that trek over the course of hundreds of years, maybe there was a god named Maui and it was he himself who spread the word. This is a myth of my own invention. A myth is a story retold many times, and I would be proud if this story of mine were retold like that. Would that all your stories should have such a fate, that they become memes, like the dance steps of the Princess Tango, in Beth's tale."

"Is that your story?" I asked, impatient.

"No, my good sir. That is my prologue. Here is my story."

Rinaldo began, "Long ago, before men learned to talk across centuries with marks on stone or on paper, the Earth itself and all its rivers and oceans and all its rocks and mountains were alive, and they delighted in the companionship of one another.

"The air above was named Maui, and he was alone.

"Then fire erupted under the ocean and dirt and rock from the depths rose to the surface, and fire and liquid rock rose in the sky, and there was dry land where before there had been boundless water. And Maui rose with the heat from the eruption and fell with the cooling of the land. And Maui loved the feel of this movement and the way these new islands scratched his back and tickled his nether parts.

"Then the day came when the Earth was struck in the midst of the ocean by a huge rock from the heavens, and the impact dislodged a chunk of what had been Earth and that chunk rose into the sky and became the moon.

"In this turmoil, Maui moved hither and thither and found himself in a new place with new islands, and he came to love those islands and the way they too scratched his back and tickled his nethers.

"The moon, by chance, settled in a fixed path moving across the sky the way the sun crossed the sky; and the ocean who had loved what was now the moon when it had been the ocean floor, reached up toward the moon as it passed overhead, then fell down in despair and rested until the moon came round again, and then the ocean rose once more.

"With these risings and fallings of the ocean, the air named Maui moved as well. And with the hot and cold that came from the movements of the sun and the changes of the seasons, Maui moved as well. Sometimes he blew to the north, and sometimes he blew to the south.

"When he blew to the north, he brushed up against the islands of Hawaii. And when he blew to the south, he brushed against New Zealand, Tahiti, Tonga, and Samoa. And he loved the islands of the north. But he also loved the islands of the south. And he did not wish to hurt either by running off to be alone with one or the other. So, he split his time, and had a time-shared love, like our bandleader Miguel. And he was faithful and predictable in his movements. And so it came to pass that men in their boats could count on the wind and navigate by where it blew and when it blew and could dare to cross vast stretches of open ocean, with confidence, following the wind-god named Maui.

"Some people settled and made homes on the islands of the north and some on the islands of the south. And all these people were one people with one blood, though they lived in lands separated by thousands of miles of open ocean. And they all worshipped and gave thanks to the god Maui."

Adolph sipped cranberry juice while savoring Rinaldo story. Then he said, "That reminds me of an ancient Chinese legend. Maybe not so ancient, since it involves Baptists, but it's got Buddhism and reincarnation.

Adolph: The Butterfly Lovers

"In a village in China," he said, "a young man and a young woman fell in love. But the man's family was strict Taoist, and the woman's family was strict Buddhist, and the parents would never allow such a marriage. The two of them vowed to each other that they would never marry anyone else and that they would live pure and righteous lives in hope that in their next reincarnation they might be united.

"They lived as they had vowed, and when they died, they were reborn. As a reward for his saintliness, the man was born into a strict Buddhist family. And as a reward for her saintliness, the woman was born into a strict Taoist family. They fell in love again, and once again they could not marry. In frustration, they lived lives of selfish dissipation, striving only for wealth and pleasure.

"This time when they died, in punishment for their many sins, they were both reborn into Baptist families. They fell in love again. And this time they married and lived happily ever after."

Harry raised his fork from his peach cobbler and volunteered again. "Before we end, I'd like to add one last thought, not a story, just a thought that Beth and I had last night looking at the stars."

Harry: One Beautiful Moment

Harry explained, "God imagined one fleeting moment a butterfly fluttering above a pond at sunset. And He created the universe, all the past and all the future, to make that one moment happen.

"Any moment, in all its detail, would require the miracle of all of creation.

"The creation of any being would require all of creation.

"Perhaps there was no beginning and will be no end, and every moment we witness the miraculous creation of everything and everyone."

Then Adolph turned to Stan, "Do you have a final story for us?"

Stan didn't hesitate.

Stan: Right of Passage

"All this talk of Japan and the South Pacific makes me think of anthropologists like Ruth Benedict and Margaret Meade, and rites of passage and the rhythm of a woman's life. Thelma and her indominable independence, her celebration of life triggered this story.

"It's a story that should have been written by a feminist fifty years ago.

"Simone wondered how she had ever gotten herself into this. Another rite of passage. Same old, same old. Blame Margaret Meade. Blame Ruth Benedict. Blame her namesake Simone de Beauvoir. Anthropology and the roots of feminism. The effort to find and record cultures with diverse female roles. All too often it came down to little more than this—a description of some remote tribe's coming of age ceremony for young girls. And this tribe wouldn't let her record either sight or sound. No laptop either because laptops have video and audio built in. Just hand-written notes. Who would care about this one ceremony among thousands of others, and even if she witnessed something unique, who would believe her account without firm evidence?

"At least she had an educated English-speaking native to explain the ceremony to her. Her informant's father was an American anthropologist. He had taken her mother and her to New York and sent her to college, after which she had married and had children. Then years later, for reasons unknown, she had returned to the village where she had been born.

"When Simone was in graduate school, she had dreamed of finding the true Amazons of the Amazon Valley, descendants of the fierce women warriors of that region who in 1542 had battled the conquistador Francisco de Orellana and for whom he had named the river, in remembrance of the Amazon warriors of ancient times. No such luck. And certainly not here. She couldn't imagine women such as these ever taking up arms.

"The ceremony might take an hour, then it would take her three hours by helicopter to get back to the city, then two hours to turn her notes into a report. She could catch a plane back to New York in the morning. Back to civilization. Another insignificant tribe checked off the ever-shrinking number of little-known cultures. Who would ever care?

"What a thankless job. What a wasted life, going through this routine over and over again. Writing reports that would only be read by a handful of others spending their lives in similar futility.

"Yes, she was able to raise grant money for these anthropological studies on gender, aging, and female identity. But she was unmarried, childless. What a waste of a life, she thought.

"Older members of the tribe had gathered in the open circle at the center of the village. But no young girls were present. No young men either. That might be worthy of note if there was a logical reason for it.

"She asked her informant, 'Where's the young girl?'

"'What young girl?'

"'The one to be initiated, the one who is now becoming a child-bearing woman, the one who is celebrating her coming of age.'

"'Why would we celebrate the start of the years of servitude? This is a ceremony of a very different kind, honoring women's rights: the right to life, the right to live her own life, free of the burdens of childbirth and child rearing and husband rearing. We are celebrating the many years of pleasure and selfhood ahead for a woman who no longer must bear children.'

"'This is a joke, right? This is your way of mocking modern civilization?'

"'You live your way. We live ours. Far be it from me to judge. We deem that when a woman has completed her years of duty to children and husband, when she is no longer obliged by nature to bear children, her real life begins. The tribe supplies her with food, lodging, and what you call *wealth* as a reward for her long years of family labor. She can do what she pleases. She can live with or bed with whomever she wishes whenever she wishes. If she wants, she can guide the tribe as a member of the Council, or she can explore her talents and her sources of pleasure as artist, as dancer, or doing whatever brings her joy. There's no limit to what she might do now that she has blossomed as her true self. These are her years of choice.'

"'*Choice*? In my world *choice* means abortion. That's choosing whether to bear a child or not.'

"'Yes, I'm well aware of the strange ways of what you call *civilization*. Here we mean real choice, the choice of how to live and with whom. You are about to witness a *Self-Ceremony*, a joyous occasion, in which we celebrate the end of the child-bearing years, the moment when a woman becomes her true self. Her marriage ends. Her responsibilities to her children end. And she chooses her own path forward, as an honored and privileged member or leader of our tribe. As Hannah Arendt might have said, had she known of our ways, the labor of a woman's life begins with childbirth and ends with menopause. Then the true work of her life, what she does for herself, begins.

"'There is no young girl here because this is my day, this is my right of passage. It is for this honor and this way of life that I returned here to my village. Perhaps you'd like to join us.'"

Everyone sat in silence, unsure whether this was another joke or a serious possibility, whether it might be good for women to celebrate menopause rather than puberty and wondering what their children might think of that.

Then Adolph announced, "As usual, we're the last ones left in the dining room. Rinaldo, we've been selfish keeping you late every night, knowing the long hours you work."

"No. I'm good sir," Rinaldo reassured him. "The pleasure has been mine. Your stories will stay fresh in my mind for many cruises to come."

"Well, spread them, please. And tell your own stories, as well. May our stories live forever, though we ourselves be far too mortal. Will you be going home soon, Rinaldo?"

"Not for another year."

"Well, *happy sails to you*, as Roy Rogers would have said if he were in the Navy. I shall be accompanying the Lady Roxanne to her doctor's office, where we shall learn the results of the biopsy face-to-face and face together whatever there is to face. And if all is well, as it should be, the two of us will be on another ship soon. I hope our paths cross again, and we have many more tales of love to share with one another.

"So, we have married off one couple, another's on their way to parenthood, and another's going to cruise forever.

"Me first, please," said Harry. "There's one more story I'd like to tell, if I may."

"The floor is yours, sir."

Harry: What Price Knowledge

"Rob time-travelled seventy years to his own future and learned that he had a wonderful life, with wife, children, grandchildren, and great grandchildren. He wrote novels that were enjoyed and revered by many. His science fiction insights into possible new technology inspired scientists to make important discoveries and led to inventions that reversed climate change. Two Noble Prize winners—one in physics and one in chemistry—eulogized him in their acceptance speeches, crediting him for the seminal ideas that guided their work. He couldn't imagine a better future.

"For his ninetieth birthday, hundreds of relatives, friends, and colleagues had gathered to celebrate his life. They would have scheduled this event for his hundredth birthday, but he had cancer—inoperable, untreatable. It had been discovered in a routine checkup. To all outward appearance, he was healthy and vigorous, amazingly so for his age. But he was expected to soon decline, dying in a few months. Brain tumor. Perhaps that slow growing tumor had altered his perception and had led to the formation of uncommon neural connections. Perhaps, without that tumor, his greatest insights would never have occurred to him.

"Rob saw all this not from the outside, like a time travelling visitor, but from the inside—in his own skin.

"In the midst of the celebration, he broke out in tears. He knew that when he returned to his present—seventy years before—due to this knowledge of the future, he would inevitably act differently, making it so this wonderful future would never happen. And he knew that this trip to his own future would only last three hours. Time was running out.

"He explained his dilemma to all who had assembled.

"They congratulated him on his creativity. They hoped he would be able to write such a novel in the little time he had left to live.

"He insisted that what he said was real. He told them, "The only solution is for me to kill myself here and now. Then I won't be able to go back and in so doing destroy this future world, despite my best intentions."

"His doctor stopped him. "Your state of mind is a side effect of your condition. It's a form of amnesia. Seventy years of your memories have been erased. In your mind, you are still a twenty-year-old college student, and the last seventy years never happened. But, in fact, everything happened just as the people here recounted and celebrated. That's all in the past and is inalterable. This is all real. You simply forgot."

"Rob laughed in relief and joy, and everyone laughed with him. They all toasted him and his wonderful life.

"Then he woke up, twenty years old, in his college dorm room. And he broke into tears, knowing that now that world, that life could never be."

Adolph laughed, applauded, then turned to me "What about you? When you've talked about yourself, it's all been about Babs and your past. What might lie in your future?"

I answered, "I don't know what the future holds. None of us do. But I can spin a story, like the other stories we've told. And this time I'll give the main character my name."

Abe: Widowed

"Two close friends, Abe and Reggie lived far away from one another. For forty years they never got together face-to-face, but they stayed in touch first by letter and then by email. After Reggie died and Abe's wife Babs died, Reggie's widow, Elle, exchanged emails with Abe. They had a lot in common as they both tried to cope with their losses. He sent her early drafts of his fiction, and she made helpful suggestions, and encouraged him. During those exchanges, Abe wished that she lived nearby. He'd like to sit down with her face-to-face and get to know her. He was attracted to her, just from her words. But he was in Connecticut and she in Chicago. He felt it wouldn't be right to woo her because she was devoted to the memory of his best friend and had no intention to ever date again. It would be a betrayal of his friend to approach her that way.

"'Elle?' he had asked Reggie, back before Reggie and Elle got married. 'What the hell. Where did she come up with a name like that? Is it short for Elizabeth or Eleanor or something else? That makes no sense as a name that parents give.' It sounded strange and made up, like Cinderella, not a real name for a real person. Then decades later the movie *Legally Blond* came out, with Reece Witherspoon playing a character named *Elle*. That made it a real name.

"Abe had only met Elle once, at their wedding, where he was the best man, and that time they had had no opportunity to talk.

"For the wedding, he flew in and out of Chicago on the same day. He was awkward and self-conscious playing the role of best man in a Jewish wedding. He wasn't Jewish and had never been to a Jewish wedding before. He didn't know anyone from either side. If he had bumped into the bride on the street the day after the wedding, without the gown and hairdo, he wouldn't have recognized her. And that was forty years ago.

"Now he was on his way to a teachers' convention in Chicago. He hadn't told Elle that he was coming, but he might give her a call when he was in town and try to get together for coffee and share memories of Reggie.

"By chance, Abe and Elle were both at LaGuardia at the same time. She had visited her sister in New Jersey and had played tourist in New York and was now about to fly home.

"They were booked on the same flight leaving at nine and getting in at midnight.

"They made eye contact sitting across from one another at the airport Starbucks, but they didn't recognize one another.

"Their seats were next to one another on the plane. There they smiled politely to one another, but still didn't recognize one another and didn't talk.

"Once in the air, when the lights went off, they both fell asleep.

"They woke up in the dark in one another's arms, both thinking that they were dreaming and that they were with their departed spouses. In the dark, they acted as they would in such a dream, hugging and groping and kissing non-stop.

"Then the lights came on, and they each realized that they had been making out with a total stranger. They separated quickly, embarrassed. They said nothing to one another. They acted as if what had happened had never happened.

"At O'Hare, they went their separate ways, never having spoken.

"The next day, Abe called Elle, and they agreed to meet at a nearby Starbucks. There, each of them was shocked to see the person from the plane. They hesitated, embarrassed. They had presumed that they would never see one another again. This coincidence was extraordinary. Abe made a tentative step toward her, and she toward him. They smiled at one another, acknowledging that they were glad to see one another again. Then they rushed into one another's arms and hugged and kissed.

"When Abe finally spoke he explained to this lady that he was here at Starbucks to meet the widow of his best friend, and she should be arriving soon. And she said that she was there to meet her late husband's best friend.

"Finally, they realized that they were there to meet one another, and they fell into one another's arms, accepting that they were fated to be together, and delighted to have such a fate."

Epilogue: To Gether

It is now the last weekend in May 2020. Minneapolis is burning. Riots and protests have broken out in other cities across the country. The tension and frustration from the pandemic and lockdown have reached a crisis point. Civil unrest can be triggered by anything and can spread faster than the virus. The social fabric of the nation is coming apart. I'm reminded of the looting and burning in the summers of the Vietnam War.

I'm writing in the midst of this crisis, not with the wisdom of hindsight. Even if it gets no worse than it is right now, much has been lost.

I'm hoping that we can *gether*. That's a word that isn't in the dictionary.

To *gether* is to find new ways to be together, new ways to meet, to bond, to love.

Even when physically isolated, I believe we can adapt and create myriad ties to others. We can come together in spirit, to share experiences and emotions to the point that we are intimately connected.

Perhaps the virus will mutate to become less virulent, or we will have an effective vaccine. In that case, you will be able to read these stories from an ironic perspective, knowing that the world returned to the *old normal* and my speculation about what was lost was overreaction.

May that be so.

In any case, may we always treasure our *normal life*, knowing, as we now know, that it is fragile and should never be taken for granted.

About the Author

Richard lives in Milford, CT, where he writes fiction full-time. He worked for DEC, the minicomputer company, as writer and Internet evangelist. He graduated from Yale, with a major in English, went to Yale graduate school in Comparative Literature, and earned an MA in Comparative Literature from the U. of Massachusetts at Amherst. At Yale, he studied creative writing with Robert Penn Warren and Joseph Heller.

To Gether Tales and Richard's five previous novels also published by All Things That Matter Press (*Parallel Lives, Beyond the 4th Door, Nevermind, Breeze,* and *Shakespeare's Twin Sister*) can be read in any order. They are independent stories, with overlapping themes and styles. Each novel presents a different view of reality, a different way of trying to understand the mysteries of life.

His other published works include: *The Name of Hero* (historical novel), *Ethiopia Through Russian Eyes* (translation from Russian), *The Lizard of Oz* (satiric fantasy), *Now and Then and Other Tales from Ome* (children's stories), and five pioneering books about Internet business. His web site is seltzerbooks.com